Timid Lucy

by

Sarah Schoonmaker Baker

Double 9 BOOKS

Timid Lucy
by Sarah Schoonmaker Baker

ISBN: 978-93-69073-06-1

Published by

DOUBLE 9 BOOKS

2/13-B, Ansari Road
Daryaganj, New Delhi – 110002
info@double9books.com
www.double9books.com
Tel. 011-40042856

ABOUT THE AUTHOR

Sarah Schoonmaker Baker was an author best known for her contributions to children's literature. Her works predominantly explore themes of emotional growth, family bonds, and moral lessons. Baker's writing often delves into the struggles of young characters, particularly girls, as they face personal challenges like fear, insecurity, and loss. In her stories, the characters' journeys towards self-acceptance are guided by love, kindness, and the support of their families. Baker's books, such as Little Tora, The Swedish Schoolmistress and Other Stories, Aunt Friendly's Picture Book, The Golden House, and Timid Lucy, all share a focus on personal transformation. Whether it's through the nurturing of a schoolmistress in Little Tora, the moral guidance provided in Aunt Friendly's Picture Book, or the introspective journey of Timid Lucy, her works are characterized by their emotional depth and simple yet powerful lessons. Her writing is gentle but insightful, aiming to nurture both the minds and hearts of her readers. Baker's books were cherished for their portrayal of everyday life and how personal growth, family support, and love can help individuals overcome their challenges. Sarah Schoonmaker Baker's legacy as a writer remains rooted in her ability to craft stories that teach, uplift, and inspire.

CONTENTS

CHAPTER I
THE LITTLE BED-ROOM

Dr. Vale had the prettiest house in all Chatford. It was a tasteful, white cottage, with a green lawn in front, and tall elm trees about it. The side windows looked out upon a pleasant orchard, where the smooth, ripe apples peeped temptingly from their beds of fresh leaves. At one of these windows there was a neat curtain, that was looped back one summer evening, while through the open casement there floated the perfume of the rose bush that had climbed the cottage wall, until its buds could look in at the upper window. A pretty sight there was within! the moonlight streamed on the floor, and lit up as sweet a little bed-room as any fairy could desire. The small counterpane and bureau-cover were white as snow, on the tiny work-table there was a vase of fresh flowers, and the miniature book-case was filled with an interesting collection of nicely-bound volumes. There was nothing wanting to give the apartment an air of perfect taste and comfort.

Did the young owner enjoy that pleasant room? Young she must have been, for everything, even to the low rocking-chair, was evidently prepared for the use of some favoured child.

Presently the door opened, but no one entered. Lucy Vale, the doctor's youngest daughter, stood timidly without. Surely there was nothing frightful in that quiet room? yet she did not venture in until the light was so steady that she could see plainly into its farthest corners. As soon, as she had locked the door behind her, she looked into the closet, behind the curtain, under the bed, and even under the bureau, where nothing thicker than a turtle could possibly have hidden itself.

There had not been a robbery in the peaceful village of Chatford in the memory of the oldest inhabitant, so there was no danger of Lucy's disturbing any villain in his hiding-place. If she had chanced to find the thief she seemed so earnestly seeking, she would have been in a most unfortunate position, as her bed-room door was locked, and, without any weapon, her feeble arm would have been but poor protection.

Children who never go to sleep without hunting for robbers, seldom think what they would do if they should at last succeed in finding one, nicely stowed away in a closet. Few thieves are so hardened as to injure a sleeping child, while the most cowardly might be led to strike a blow on being suddenly discovered, and placed in danger of punishment. After all, even if there were thieves in a house, the safest course for a child would be to go quietly to sleep, and leave the evil men to steal and depart.

Lucy Vale did not seem quite satisfied with her first search; again she furtively glanced about, before she sat down to read the chapter in the Bible, which she had been taught never to omit at night. Lucy read her Bible as a duty, not because she loved it, or wished to learn the will of God, and now she could not fix her attention at all upon its sacred pages.

She was hardly seated when a slight sound in the orchard attracted her notice; she jumped up and ran to the window. All was quiet in that peaceful scene, save the occasional dropping of the ripe fruit. The shadows of the leaves quivered in the moonlight in what seemed to her a mysterious manner; a strange feeling of fear stole over her; she did not return to the Bible, but having hastily undressed, she fell upon her knees for her evening prayer. Lucy would have thought it very wicked to go to sleep without what she called saying her prayers. In truth it was only *saying* them, for while she repeated the solemn words, her thoughts were far away. Sometimes she would get so busily thinking of other things, that her lips would cease to move, and she would remain on her knees, buried in thought, for many minutes. As soon as she remembered why she was kneeling, she would hurry over the remainder of her prayers and go to bed, quite satisfied that she had done her duty.

On this particular evening her prayers were soon over, and she was quickly in bed, leaving the lamp burning; its light however was of but little use to her, as she thrust her head under the covering, hardly leaving space enough to breathe through.

If Mrs. Maxwell, the housekeeper, had known that Lucy kept her light burning at night, she would have scolded her severely, for she often said, "it was flying in the face of nature to try to make night like day, and for her part she thought it downright wicked to be wasting oil when everybody was asleep, to say nothing of the danger of fire."

Dr. Vale had lost his wife when Lucy was just six years old, and since that time Mrs. Maxwell had been his housekeeper; he trusted everything to her, and she seemed to take the greatest delight in being economical, that none of her master's substance might be wasted. She was not bad-tempered, but she had a stern, harsh manner, and was easily worried by children, only thinking them good when they were silent and stirred neither hand nor foot. Lucy seldom came near her without being blamed for something, or told to sit down and be quiet.

The little girl would have been quite lonely had it not been for her brother Hartwell, who was just two years older than herself. Lucy was now ten, but Hartwell seemed to think her a very little child, hardly fit to be his companion, yet he would sometimes permit her to play with him, and a dearly-bought pleasure it was. Harty, as he was generally called, was indolent; he could not bear to move about, and therefore found it very convenient to have Lucy to wait upon him. He never seemed to have thought his sister might not like running up and down stairs any better than he did. It was so easy when he wanted anything to tell Lucy to run for it, that sometimes he kept her little feet in such constant motion that at night she was quite tired out. If she ever complained, he told her, girls were made to wait on boys, and if she could not do such trifles for him she had better go to her doll-baby and not be about in his way. Lucy loved her brother, and liked to be near him, so she seldom refused to do what he asked her, although he often called her disobliging when she had been trying her best to please him.

Hartwell was very fond of teasing, and his poor little sister had to suffer for his amusement. Sometimes he would make her cry, by telling her that she was so ugly that it was painful to look at her; at others he would call her a coward, and run after her to put insects on her neck, or he would jump out from a dark corner and shout in her ear when she thought herself quite alone.

As you will conclude, Lucy did not lead a very happy life. Her father was so constantly occupied that he seldom took his meals with the family, and sometimes hardly spoke to his little daughter for days together. She had no one to whom she could talk freely; Mrs. Maxwell never listened to her, and her brother was so apt to laugh at what she said, that she did not dare to tell him many things that troubled her. She was naturally a timid child, but since her mother's death she had grown so bashful that she could hardly answer when a stranger spoke to her. Many of her childish fears, which a kind friend in the beginning could easily have banished, had become so strong that she lived in perpetual alarm.

CHAPTER II
THE THUNDER-SHOWER

About midnight Lucy was roused by a loud clap of thunder. The rain was dashing in through the open window, and the waning lamp seemed but a spark amid the almost incessant flashes of lightning. The poor child trembled with fear, she dared not close the window, and yet the flying drops almost reached her little bed. She lay in an agony of terror, thinking that every moment might be her last. The idea of death was horrible to her: in broad daylight, or when pleasantly occupied, she could forget that she must die; but any sudden fright would bring the solemn truth to her mind and fill her with distress. She had never heard Mrs. Maxwell or Harty speak of being afraid of death, and dared not mention her fear to them, and with her father she was so shy, that he knew very little of what was passing in her mind.

The many faults of which she had been guilty rose to her mind in that awful storm, and she resolved if her life were spared never to do wrong again. After making this resolution she felt a little comforted, and began to think what could be done about the window. She got up and took the lamp to go and call some one to her assistance. But whom should she call? "I will not disturb father," she said to herself, "he was so very tired last night; Harty will laugh at me for not doing it myself; and Mrs. Maxwell—I cannot wake her, she will be so very angry." Thus thinking, she stood irresolutely in the hall, starting at every flash of lightning, and afraid either to go forward or return. Just then Mrs. Maxwell opened her door: "What are you about there?" said she, with an astonished look at Lucy.

"Please, ma'am," said the little girl, who was really glad to see a human face, "will you shut my window?"

"Why in the name of wonder did not you shut it yourself?" was the response. Lucy was silent, and they entered the room, together. "A pretty piece of work!" said the neat housekeeper, holding tip both hands, as her eyes fell on the soaking carpet. She shut the window hastily, and then said to Lucy, "Come to my room, for it wouldn't be safe for any one to sleep in that damp place."

Lucy was so much afraid of Mrs. Maxwell, that it was quite a trial to be in the same bod with her; she crept close to the wall, not daring to go to sleep, lest she should be restless, and wake the stern woman at her side. She had many serious thoughts that night, and again and again resolved never more to do wrong.

Towards morning she had a pleasant nap, from which she was roused by the morning bell. The sun was shining cheerfully into the room, and the wild storm of the night seemed like a painful dream. She dressed herself carefully, and knelt to say her morning prayer, simple words which she had repeated a thousand times with as little thought as if they had been without sense or meaning. Those same words, spoken with earnest sincerity, would have called down a blessing from Him who loves to listen when children truly pray. Lucy had not forgotten her resolution to do right, but she trusted in her own feeble efforts.

A flush of pleasure lit the usually pale face of the little girl as she saw her father seated at the breakfast-table. She glided into the chair next him, and hardly ate anything, she was so busily occupied in watching his plate, and placing all he might need beside him. Harty, meanwhile, showed his delight in his father's company by being more talkative than usual. He had taken a long walk in the fresh morning air, and had many things to tell about what he had seen. What had interested him most was a tall tree, which the recent lightning had struck and splintered from the topmost bough to the root.

Lucy shuddered as the conversation brought the painful scene of the night afresh to her mind. It revived Mrs. Maxwell's memory also, for she turned to Lucy with a stern look, and said, "How came you with a light last night?"

Lucy blushed, and hastily answered, "I forgot to put it out when I went to bed."

"Careless child!" was Mrs. Maxwell's only reply; but nothing that she could have said would have made Lucy more unhappy than the fault she had just committed. What would she not have given, a few moments after, to recall those false words; but they had been spoken, and recorded in the book of God!

During breakfast Dr. Vale looked anxiously many times at the little girl at his side. There was nothing of cheerful childhood in her appearance; her slender figure was slightly bent, and her small face was pale and thin; her eyes were cast down, and she only occasionally looked up timidly from under the long lashes. Her little mouth was closed too tightly, and her whole expression was so sad and subdued, that he was truly troubled about it. It was plain to any one who looked at her that she was not happy.

The doctor dearly loved his children. Harty he could understand, but Lucy was a mystery to him. He felt certain that she loved him, for she never disobeyed him, and when he was with her she was sure to nestle at his side, and take his hand in hers; but she seldom talked to him, and was growing daily more silent and shy.

"Something must be done for her," he inwardly said. His thoughts were interrupted by Harty's calling out, "Why don't you eat something, Lucy? There, let me butter the baby some bread." Rude as this remark seemed, it was meant in kindness.

"I don't want anything, Harty," answered the sister. "Nonsense!" said he; "you are thin enough already: one of the boys asked me the other day, if my sister fed on broom-splinters, for she looked like one;" and the thoughtless boy gave a loud laugh.

It would have been much better for Lucy if she could have laughed too, but the tears filled her eyes, and she pettishly replied, "I should not care what I was, if it was only something that could not be laughed at."

At this Harty only shouted the louder. "Hush, Harty," said Dr. Vale; "for shame, to tease your sister. Don't mind him, Lucy," and he drew his arm tenderly around her. She laid her head on his lap, and cried bitterly. This kindness from her father would usually have made her quite happy, but now the falsehood she had first uttered made her feel so guilty that she could not bear his gentle manner. She longed to tell him all—her fault of the morning, her terror of the night before—all she had thought and suffered for so many weary days; but her lips would not move, and she only continued to sob. A ring at the bell called the father away, or she might have gained courage to open her heart to him. If Lucy could have been more with him, she would have found a friend who would have listened to all her little trials, and given her the truest consolation and advice. It was a source of sorrow to Dr. Vale that he could be so little with his family, and on this particular morning he felt it with unusual force.

"My little daughter is going on badly," he said to himself, as he entered his chaise, to make his round of visits. "The child is losing all her spirits; she needs a different companion from Harty; he is too boisterous, too much of a tease for my little flower. Mrs. Maxwell is not the person to make a child cheerful; I must have Rosa at home." The doctor was prompt to act when he had fixed upon a plan, and that day a letter was written to his eldest daughter, recalling her home. For three years before her mother's death, and since that time, Rosa had been under the care of her uncle, the Rev. Mr. Gillette. This gentleman had been obliged by ill-health to give up the exercise of his holy profession, but he did not cease to devote himself to his Master's cause. He received a few young ladies into his family, whose education he conducted with all the earnestness of a father. His chief aim was to lead his pupils in the pleasant paths of virtue, and make them to know and love the Lord. Rosa, as the child of his departed sister, had been peculiarly dear to him; he had spared no pains in moulding her character, and was now beginning to see the fruits of his labour in the daily improvement of his attractive niece. To Rosa, then, whom we shall soon know better, the doctor's letter was immediately sent.

Lucy, meanwhile, had no idea of the change that was soon to take place in her home. She passed a sad day, for the remembrance of the untruth she had spoken hung about her like a dark cloud. She had been taught that a lie was hateful to God, and sure to bring punishment. Mrs. Maxwell had made it a part of her duty to hear Lucy recite the Catechism every Sunday. These were trying times to the little girl, for the eye of the questioner was constantly fixed upon her; and if she failed or faltered in one of the long answers, she was sent to her room to study there until she could go through the part without hesitation. Mrs. Maxwell generally closed the Sunday evening exercise by telling Lucy how dreadful a thing it was to be a bad child, and that God saw her every moment, and would punish every wicked act she committed. From these conversations Lucy would go away in tears, resolved never to do wrong again; but these resolutions soon passed from her mind, until recalled by some fright or by the lesson of the next Sunday evening.

She only thought of God as an awful Judge, who would take delight in punishing her, and was far happier when she could forget Him.

CHAPTER III
THE MEDICINE

The morning light streamed pleasantly into Lucy's pretty room, and there was the little girl quite dressed, and moving about as busily as Mrs. Maxwell herself. She had been up since the dew-drops began to sparkle in the sunlight. She could not make up her mind to confess her fault to her father or Mrs. Maxwell, but she was determined to be so very good as to quite make up for it. In the first place, she would put her room in order; that would please Mrs. Maxwell.

With a tremendous effort she turned her little bed, and then spread up the clothes with the greatest care. It was her first attempt in that way, and not very successful, but she was quite satisfied with it, and walked about surveying it as if it had been a masterpiece of housewifery.

The doctor was again at the breakfast-table, and he was pleased to see his little daughter looking so much more cheerful. Harty, as usual, was in excellent spirits; but his father's rebuke was still fresh in his mind, and he refrained from teasing his sister, and contented himself with telling funny stories about school occurrences, until even Mrs. Maxwell was forced to laugh.

As they rose from the table, Dr. Vale handed Lucy a small parcel, saying, "Take good care of this, my dear, and leave it at Mrs. Tappan's on your way to school; it is some medicine for her, which she will need at ten o'clock. I have a long ride to take in another direction, so good morning, my little mouse." Having kissed her affectionately, he jumped into his chaise, and was soon out of sight.

Lucy was unusually happy when she started for school; Harty had not teased her, Mrs. Maxwell had not found fault with her, and her father had trusted her with something to do for him.

The summer sky was clear above her, and her feet made not a sound as she tripped over the soft grass. The wild rose bushes offered her a sweet bouquet, and she plucked a cluster of buds as she passed. In the pleasure of that bright morning, Lucy forgot her good resolutions. She did not think of her kind Heavenly Father while enjoying His beautiful world. Fear alone brought Him to her mind: she remembered Him in the storm, but forgot Him in the sunshine.

Lucy was soon at Mrs. Tappan's gate, and was raising the latch, when the large house-dog came down the walk and stood directly in the way. She thought he looked very fierce, and did not dare to pass him. She walked on a short distance and then came back, hoping he would be gone; but no, he had not moved an inch. While she was doubting what to do, the school-bell rang; thrusting the parcel into her pocket, she hurried on, saying to herself, "As it is so late, I am sure father will not blame me."

She was hardly seated in school, however, before she began to be troubled about what she had done. "Perhaps Mrs. Tappan was very ill," she thought; the shutters were all closed, and her father had called there twice the day before, and had already seen her that morning. With such thoughts in her mind, of course Lucy did not learn her lesson; although she held the book in her hand, and seemed to have her eyes fixed upon it. When she was called up to recite, she blundered, hesitated, and utterly failed. The tears now filled her eyes. Glancing at the clock, she saw that it yet wanted a quarter of ten.

"Please, Miss Parker, may I go home?" she asked.

"Are you unwell?" asked the teacher, kindly.

"No," murmured Lucy.

"Then go to your seat," said Miss Parker, a little sternly; "and never ask me again to let you go home unless you have a good reason."

"I wouldn't mind her, she's as cross as she can be," whispered Julia Staples, as she took her seat at Lucy's side.

Lucy knew Miss Parker was not cross, yet she felt a little comforted by Julia's seeming interested in her trouble, and placed her hand in hers under the desk, as if to thank her new friend; for Julia Staples had seldom spoken to her before.

Wearily the hours of school passed away. At last the clock struck one, and the children were dismissed. Lucy was hurrying off, when Julia Staples called after her to wait, for she was going that way. Lucy did not like to be disobliging, and therefore stood still until her companion was quite ready.

"I hate school, don't you?" said Julia, as they walked along.

Now Lucy did not hate school, she generally found it very pleasant; but she thought it would seem childish to say so to a large girl like Julia Staples; so she answered, rather awkwardly, "Yes, I did not like it to-day."

"I can't bear Miss Parker," continued Julia, "she's so partial; I know you don't like her, from the way you looked at her this morning."

Lucy did like Miss Parker, for she had often drawn the little girl to her side, and spoken very tenderly to her, more tenderly than any one had done since her own mother's death, and she was therefore glad that they came that moment to the road which led to Julia's home, for there they must part.

"Good morning," said Julia, not waiting for an answer; "I shall call for you to-morrow," and Lucy went on her way alone. She had been almost led to speak unkindly of a person she really loved, because she was afraid to say boldly what was in her mind.

As she came in sight of Mrs. Tappan's quiet house, she saw her father coming out of the gate, looking thoughtfully on the ground. He did not see her, and she had to run very fast to overtake him before he got into his chaise.

"Father! dear father!" she said, "do stop a minute; is Mrs. Tappan very ill? Do not be angry with me, here is the medicine."

The doctor looked quite serious while Lucy told him of her fright in the morning, and her sorrow after she reached school at not having delivered the medicine. The dreaded dog was standing within the gate while they were talking without; the doctor called him and made Lucy look into his mild eye and pat him gently. "You see, my dear," said the father, as the hand of the little girl rested on the head of the quiet animal, "that you need not have been afraid of Rover. You should have remembered that in not delivering the medicine you might be doing more harm to another than the dog would have done to you. Even after you were at school, all might have been well if you had had the courage to tell the whole truth to your teacher; she would certainly have excused you. I cannot say what will be the consequence of your foolish timidity. Mrs. Tappan is very ill!"

As her father spoke these words, Lucy's tears fell fast. Not another syllable was spoken until they reached home. Harty came out to meet them, calling out to his sister, "Are those red eyes the sign of bad lessons?" She made him no reply, but hastened to her room to think on her own folly, and poor Mrs. Tappan.

It was a long afternoon to the little girl; her dinner was sent to her, and she remained alone until dark. This was the day which had commenced so pleasantly, and in which Lucy had intended to please everybody. Alas! the poor child had not asked God's help to enable her to do her duty, nor had she been faithful in her own exertions.

When the tea-bell rang, she hastened down stairs, hoping to hear from her father good news about Mrs. Tappan, but he did not appear. Harty seeing his sister look so unhappy, forbore to tease her, and the meal passed over in silence. Eight o'clock came, and Mrs. Maxwell gave Lucy her light, and told her to go to bed. She did not dare to ask to sit up a little longer, for she knew the request would not be granted. Feeling like a criminal, the little girl went to her room—that pretty room, how many unhappy hours she had passed there! but none more wretched than on that evening.

In vain she tried to sleep. Whenever she closed her eyes, the form of the sick woman would rise before her, and she could almost fancy she heard her groans. Nine o'clock struck, and ten, yet Lucy was awake. About eleven she heard the street-door open; then there was a careful step upon the stairs, and some one moved towards the doctor's room. She was out of bed in an instant, and hastening towards the door. It was locked as usual, and before she could open it, her father had passed. She almost flew along the passage, and sought his arm as he was entering his room. He clasped her to his breast and kissed her tenderly, saying at the same time, what she so much wished to hear, "Thank God, Mrs. Tappan is out of danger. You ought to be very grateful," he continued, "my dear child, that your fault has led to no evil; I trust that this will teach you not to let childish fears lead you to neglect your duty!" Much relieved she returned to her own room, but no thanks were uplifted from her young heart to Him who had been pleased to spare the stroke of death.

CHAPTER IV
AN ANNOUNCEMENT

All the family at the cottage were awake at sunrise the next morning, and there was an unusual bustle throughout the house. Mrs. Maxwell was flying about with a duster in her hand, giving her orders to the servants, and working twice as busily as any of them. The large room opposite to Lucy's was open, and being put in thorough order. This room had been occupied by Lucy's mother during her illness, and had been kept closed since her death. It had always seemed a gloomy place to the little girl; she had peeped in when the door chanced to be open to air the apartment. Now it was undergoing an entire change; the shutters, so long fastened, were thrown back, and muslin curtains fluttered in the morning breeze; neat covers had been placed on the dark bureau and table; and on the latter Mrs. Maxwell was placing a large India work-box that had belonged to Mrs. Vale, and which Lucy had not seen since she was a very little child.

Before going down to breakfast, she stepped in to see the pleasant change more closely; she was startled by meeting a mild glance from a sweet face on the wall. It was her mamma's portrait that looked thus gently upon her, and she almost expected the kind face to bend down to kiss her, as it had been wont to do when that dear mamma was alive. Lucy had never seen this picture before, and she could not help wondering where it had come from, and why it was placed there, where none of the family could see it. Indeed, she was thoroughly puzzled to understand what could be the cause of all this commotion in the usually quiet house.

Mrs. Maxwell poured out coffee in silence, and Lucy asked no questions; but before they rose from the table, Harty came bounding into the room, crying, "Guess who is coming here, Lucy."

"Isn't it cousin Jack?" asked Lucy, almost sighing to think what a life she should lead with the two boys to tease her.

"Guess again," said Harty; and she did guess all the aunts, cousins, and friends that had ever been to make them a visit, but in vain. When Harty had enjoyed her curiosity long enough, he said, "Well, Miss Mouse" (a name he often called her), "sister Rosa is coming home to live, and she is to tell us what to do, and be like a little mother for us! That's what father told me."

Lucy did not know whether to be glad or sorry at this news; she had not seen her sister for many years, and perhaps she might be afraid of her, and perhaps Rosa might not care for such a little girl as herself, even younger than Harty.

The excited boy was in a state of great delight, and he talked to Lucy until she quite entered into his feelings. "Won't it be nice," he said, "to have Rosa at home? I shall offer her my arm when she goes to church, and lead you with the other hand. I shall lend her my 'Swiss Family Robinson;' I mean to put it in her room, that she may read it whenever she pleases. But she need not attempt to make me mind her, for I sha'n't do it; I am not going to have any girl set over me!"

"Oh, fie! Harty!" said Lucy, "to speak so of sister Rosa before you have seen her."

"Before I have seen her!" repeated Harty; "I remember her perfectly; I have not forgotten how I used to play—she was my horse—and drive her round the house; you were only a little baby then."

"Not so very little," answered Lucy, pettishly, for her brother had made her feel as if it were a disgrace to be young.

While they were talking, Julia Staples called to walk with her to school. Lucy soon told her all about her sister's expected return.

"I should not think you would like it!" said Julia; "she'll want the nicest of everything for herself, and make you wait on her, as if you were her servant."

Before they reached the school-house, Lucy was quite sure that Rosa's coming would make her unhappy. Julia Staples had been talking with little thought, but she had roused evil feelings in Lucy's mind which were strangers there. She was not naturally envious, but now her heart burned at the idea that her sister would always be praised, and go out with her father, while she would be left at home with no one to care for her. Children do not think enough of the harm they may do each other by idle conversation. Julia might have encouraged Lucy in feeling kindly towards her expected sister, and have made her look forward to the meeting with pleasure; but she filled her mind with wicked, envious thoughts.

Do my young friends ever think whether they have roused wrong feelings in their companions? Two children can hardly talk together for half an hour without having some influence over each other, for good or for evil. The wrong thought that you have planted in the heart of a child may strengthen, and lead her to do some very wicked thing when you have forgotten the conversation.

A traveller once took some seeds of a very valuable plant with him on a journey. From time to time he cast them in the fields as he passed, and when he was far away they sprang up and were a great blessing to the people who owned the fields. A wicked traveller might have scattered the seeds of poisonous plants, which would have grown up to bring sickness and death to all who partook of them. Our life is like a journey, and whenever we talk with the people around us, we cast some seeds in their hearts, those which may spring up to bless them, or those which may cause them sin and sorrow.

CHAPTER V
THE ARRIVAL

"Your sister is to be here at ten o'clock, and you must be ready to receive her," said Mrs. Maxwell to Lucy, a few days after the occurrences related in the last chapter.

"Shall I put on my white frock?" asked Lucy.

"Nonsense! child," was the reply; "isn't your sister to see you every day, from morning to night, in whatever you happen to have on? Go, get a clean apron, and make your hair smooth, that is all the dressing that little girls need."

This idea did not suit Lucy, for she was very anxious that her sister should love her, and she thought if she were prettily dressed at first, she would be more likely to do so. As she looked in the glass while arranging her hair, she thought she never had seemed quite so ugly. The fact was, she was beginning to have a fretful expression, which was spoiling her face. Lucy had never heard that scowls must in time become wrinkles. She was not at all pleased with her simple appearance, but there seemed no way for her to wear any ornament, not even a hair ribbon, for her soft light curls were cut so closely, that they could only lie like her waxen doll's, in golden rings about her head.

Lucy was fond of dress, and she would have liked to wear jewellery to school, as many of the scholars did, but Mrs. Maxwell never allowed it. The little girl had a bracelet of her mother's hair, and this she, one morning, clasped on her arm under her apron, to be worn on the outside after she reached school, where Mrs. Maxwell could not see it. As she stopped on the road to change it, there came a sudden pang into her heart—she was deceiving, and with the gift of her dead mother; perhaps that dear mother could see her now, she thought; and hastily putting down her sleeve, she hurried to school.

Though the bracelet was not displayed, and no one around her knew that she wore it, she felt guilty and unhappy until it was restored to the box in which it was usually kept. The remembrance of that day checked her this morning, as she was about to place on her slender finger a ring which had been her mother's, and in her child-like dress, she went down to wait for her sister.

She found Harty at the front window, but by no means in a fit condition to give Rosa a welcome, for his face had not been washed since breakfast, and his dark curls were, as usual, in wild confusion.

"Here comes Miss Prim!" he shouted, as Lucy entered, "as neat as a new pin. For my part, I don't intend to dress up for Rosa; she'll have to see me this way, and she may as well get used to it at once. I do wish she'd come, I am tired of waiting; the clock struck ten five minutes ago. Hurrah! there's the carriage!" he cried, and was out of the room in an instant.

Lucy longed to follow, but she seemed fastened to her chair; there she sat, looking anxiously out of the window, as the carriage entered the yard and drove up to the door.

Her father got out first, and then gave his hand to a tall, slender girl, who sprang with one leap to the stops, and was locked in Harty's rough embrace.

"But where is little Lucy?" she asked, when Harty had ceased to smother her with kisses.

The voice was kind and cheerful, and Lucy stepped forward, hanging her head, and timidly putting out her hand.

Rosa overlooked the little hand, and clasped the bashful child tenderly in her arms.

Tears came in Lucy's eyes, she could not tell why—not because she was unhappy, for she felt sure she should love her sister.

"God bless you, my children!" said Dr. Vale, "may you be happy together. Rosa, you must be a second mother to our little one. Lucy, show your sister her room; I must leave you now; I must not neglect my patients, even to enjoy seeing my children once more together." So saying, he drove from the door.

Rosa's room had no gloomy associations to her, for she had not been at home at the time of her mother's death, and she only remembered it as the spot where she had enjoyed much sweet conversation with that dear mother, now, she trusted, a saint in heaven.

As her eyes fell on the truthful picture of that lost friend, they were dimmed by natural tears, which were soon wiped away, for why should she weep for one whose pure spirit was at rest?

Rosa was a Christian; not that she never did wrong, but it was her chief wish to do right. She had just been confirmed, and felt most anxious to do something to serve the Saviour, whose follower she had professed herself to be. When she received her father's letter recalling her home, she found it hard to obey, for she had been so long at her uncle's, that it was a severe trial to leave his family circle, and to lose his advice, which she knew she should so much need, to keep her true to the promises which she had now taken upon herself. Mr. Gillette, with gentle firmness, pointed out to his niece that it was her plain duty to return unhesitatingly to her father's house.

"You wish, dear Rosa," he said, "to be a true follower of the Saviour, and to do something for His cause. Go home to your brother and sister, strive by example and kind advice to lead their young hearts to Him who will repay all their love. But be careful, my child, while you are striving for the good of others, not to neglect your own character. Be yourself all that you wish to make them!"

Rosa had returned with a true desire to be of service to Lucy and Harty, and she had many plans for their welfare. Just now she longed to be alone for a few moments, that she might thank her Heavenly Father for His protecting care during the journey, and ask His blessing on her new home.

Her first impulse was to send the children away, but she checked it, and made them quite happy by allowing them to assist her in unpacking. Lucy handled everything very carefully, but Harty made Rosa tremble, by his way of tumbling over her collars and ribbons.

At last, all was unpacked but the little box of books, which Harty insisted on opening himself. "Run, get my hatchet," he said to Lucy, who willingly brought it.

"This is too small to work with," said the eager boy, after a few moments' exertion, "get me the large hatchet, Lucy."

Lucy again obeyed; but her brother spoke not a word of thanks when she came back, breathless with running. This rudeness did not escape Rosa, although she hoped it was only occasioned by her brother's anxiety to oblige her, and was not his usual manner.

The obstinate nails at last came out, and all the party sat down on the floor, and began taking out the books. Harty looked at the titles one after the other, and threw them aside with disappointment; at length he said, impatiently, "Are they all as sober as sermons? I should think you were going to be a parson, Rosa."

"Not exactly!" said she, with a merry laugh, "but you must not be surprised if I preach a little sometimes. Then you don't like my books; I am sorry for that, but I hope we shall have a great deal of pleasure in reading them together, by-and-by.”

“Not I,” answered Harty; “I like stories about shipwrecks and great soldiers, and strange and wonderful things.”

“Then here is a book which ought to please you,” said Rosa, laying her hands on the beautiful Bible which had been Mr. Gillette’s parting gift. “Do you not love to read it?”

Harty hung his head, and answered, “There are no nice stories in the Bible.”

“No nice stories in the Bible!” said Rosa. She turned the leaves rapidly, and began to read the story of Gideon. At first, Harty looked very indifferent; but she read in a clear voice, and animated manner, and by degrees he dropped the books which lay on his lap, and leaned his head on his hands, in rapt attention. When she came to the attack on the camp of the Midianites, he was ready to join the shout, “The sword of the Lord and of Gideon!” “Where is it? where is it?” asked Harty, when Rosa had finished, “I want to look at it myself.”

She pointed to the place, and promised to find him many more interesting stories, that they could read together.

Lucy meanwhile had crept close to Rosa’s side, and laid her hand upon her lap. “And there is something to interest you, too, Lucy,” said Rosa: “here is the Prodigal Son, let me read it to you.”

“Do! do! sister Rosa,” said both of the children. She needed no urging, and read the short and beautiful parable with real feeling.

Harty felt touched, he knew not why, but with an effort to look unconcerned, he asked, abruptly, “What does it mean, Rosa?”

“It teaches us many sweet lessons, dear Harty,” answered Rosa; “I cannot well explain them all to you, but I know that it is to make us understand that God loves us as the father loved his wandering son. Did you notice that he knew the Prodigal when he was afar off, and ran to meet him? So God sees when we wish to do right, though nobody about us may guess it, and He is ready to welcome us to His love. Is it not strange that the Holy God should love us so tenderly?”

Harty looked wearied, and did not reply. Lucy tried to speak, but she was almost weeping, and her lips would not move.

“Come, we must not talk any more,” said Rosa, cheerfully. “See how the things are all lying about. Harty, can you take the box away for me?”

He started off, with a sense of relief, and Rosa was left alone with her little sister. She kissed the child gently, and said, "You must tell me, some time, why those tears come so quickly; I want to know all that troubles you, and be your friend."

Lucy only replied by placing her hand in that of her sister. Harty now returned, and they all went to work busily, and soon arranged the books on the shelves of the bookcase.

"Come, Rosa," said Harty, "I want to show you my room, and to take you down in the orchard;" and he seized her rather forcibly by the hand.

The room was still in confusion, and Rosa would have preferred to stay and see her things nicely put away, but she contented herself with closing one or two of the drawers, and then followed her eager brother. Lucy silently went with them, keeping close to her sister's side, now and then looking half-lovingly, half-wistfully, into Rosa's cheerful face.

Harty's room was a curiosity shop, filled with all kinds of odd things that he had gathered together. Mrs. Maxwell and he had been for a long time at war about the birds' nests, nuts, shells, stones, &c., that he was constantly bringing to the house, and leaving about to her great annoyance. On several occasions she threw away his carefully collected treasures, and at last, the young gentleman, in great displeasure, went to his father and asked, "if he might not be allowed, at least in his own room, to keep anything valuable that he found in his walks." His father consented, and after that his room became a perfect museum. Stuffed birds, squirrel-skins, and crooked sticks were ranged on his mantel-piece, in a kind of order, and the chest of drawers was covered with similar specimens.

From time to time, Mrs. Maxwell came herself to dust among them, though Harty was sure to complain after such visits that his treasures had been greatly injured. On this particular morning Mrs. Maxwell had been thoroughly dusting, on account of the expected arrival, and as Harty entered the room he darted from Rosa, and carefully taking from the shelf some twigs, with bits of spiders' web attached to thorn, he angrily exclaimed, "Old Maxwell has been here, I know! I wish she would let my things alone! the hateful thing! See here, Rosa, this was a beautiful web, as perfect as it could be; I brought it only yesterday morning, when it was all strung with dew-drops, and now look at it! Isn't it enough to make any one angry?"

Rosa looked sorrowfully at her brother, and made no reply for a moment; at length she answered: "Dear Harty, you can find another spider's web; but angry words once spoken can never be taken back. Won't you show me what you have here, and forget your trouble?"

The hasty boy was soon engaged in explaining what all the queer-looking things were, and why he valued them. In some of them Rosa was much interested: she had never seen a titmouse's nest before, and as she took the curious home in her hand, she thought of the kind Heavenly Father who had taught those little creatures to build it with such skill, and had watched the nestlings from the time they left the shell, until they flew lightly away on their fluttering wings.

"What can you be thinking about?" said Harty, as she looked earnestly at the pretty thing.

"Pleasant thoughts," said Rosa, smiling, as she took from his hand a huge beetle.

Lucy wondered to see her sister take what seemed to her such a frightful thing so calmly in her hand. "There now! I like that!" shouted Harty, "she handles it like a boy. There's Lucy, she screams if I put such a thing near her, if it has been dead a month. Isn't she a goose?"

Lucy looked anxiously at Rosa, fearing she would say something unkind.

"Oh! yes, she is a little goose," was the reply, "but such a dear little goose, that I am sure I shall love her very much. We must teach her not to be afraid of trifles."

The timid child clasped Rosa's hand more closely, and inwardly resolved to try to please her sister in everything. She even touched with the tip of her finger a snake-skin from which she had always shrunk before, as she heard Harty and Rosa admiring it, while they handled it freely.

Some of the specimens which Harty seemed to think very precious were uninteresting to Rosa, and some were even disgusting; but she looked at all, and tried to discover the beauties which Harty so eagerly pointed out.

Her uncle had taught her that politeness is a Christian duty, and to be always shown, even to nearest relatives, and to those younger than ourselves.

Harty was delighted, and slapped Rosa on the back in token of his pleasure. "You are a glorious girl!" said Harty; "why, if that had been Lucy, she would have cried, and said I always hurt her."

"You forget," said Rosa, "that Lucy is a delicate little girl; you cannot play with her as you would with a boy. You must take care of her, as the knights of old guarded their ladye-love, and handle her as carefully as you would a bird's nest."

At this Harty laughed, and Lucy smiled.

"Now for the orchard," cried Harty; and away he ran, pulling the girls so rapidly along that they could hardly keep from falling down stairs.

A pleasant place was that orchard; the grass was fresh and short, and some of the branches of the old trees bent almost to the ground. Under these Harty had placed wooden seats, and there it was his delight to study. Very little studying he accomplished, though, for his eye wandered at one moment to a ripe apple on the topmost bough, and the next to a curious insect that was creeping on the trunk near him.

Rosa placed herself on the rustic seat, and looked upward through the waving branches to the clear blue sky above, and a half smile came over her face, that Harty did not understand. He did not guess that the sweet scene was filling the heart of his sister with love to the great Creator. Nor did Lucy understand her any better; but the expression on her sister's countenance made her warm with love towards her.

Harty soon grew restless, and engaged his companions for a race. Away they flew over the soft grass, and Rosa was the first to reach the fence, which had been agreed upon as the goal; Lucy came next, while Harty, puffing and panting, brought up the rear.

"I declare that was not fair," he began; "we did not start together."

"Never mind," said Rosa; "we girls ought to be the fastest runners, for that is all we can do in danger. Girls run, while boys must stand and defend themselves and their sisters."

This view of the case suited Harty, and reconciled him to his defeat; and they continued chatting amicably in the orchard and piazza until the bell rang for them to prepare for dinner. As they entered the house, Mrs. Maxwell met them, and looking sternly at Rosa, she said, "I hoped you were going to set a good example, Miss Rosa, to these careless children, but there I found your room all in confusion, while you were out running races. Your father has reckoned without his host, if he looks to you to make them particular."

Rosa knew that it had cost her an effort to leave the room in that condition, and that she had done so to please her brother. She did not defend herself, however, for she now saw that it would have been better to make him wait a few moments. Hastening up stairs, she soon found a place for everything, and put everything in its place, and as she did so, she resolved not to let her anxiety to win the affection of her brother and sister lead her astray.

Dr. Vale looked very happy, when he sat down to dinner with his family about him. He was pleased with Rosa's easy, cheerful manner, and delighted to see Lucy's face lighted with smiles, and Harty doing his best to act the gentleman. And acting it was, for anything like politeness was far from being habitual with him.

When they rose from the table, Dr. Vale led his eldest daughter to her room, and entering it, closed the door. The doctor walked towards the portrait, and gazed at it a few moments in silence, then, turning to Rosa, he said, with some emotion, "You do not, I fear, remember your mother distinctly, my child. I have had this life-like image of your mother placed where it will be ever near you, that it may remind you of the part that you must act to the dear children. May God bless and assist you in your task: pray earnestly to Him to watch over you and guide you, and you cannot fail. And now, dearest, never think me cold nor stern, when I am silent. My professional cares often weigh so heavily upon me that I notice but little what is passing around me; but nothing can so absorb my mind as to make me indifferent to the welfare of my children. Come to me with all that troubles you, and you shall find a father's heart, though perhaps a faltering tongue."

The doctor pressed his daughter to his bosom, kissed her forehead, and left the room. As soon as he had gone, Rosa fell on her knees to implore the God of all good to strengthen her for the great task that was before her, and to enable her to make herself such an example as the children might safely follow.

CHAPTER VI
AN ACCIDENT

In about half an hour there was a gentle tap at Rosa's door. It was Lucy, who entered timidly, and going towards Rosa, said, blushing, "Don't mind Mrs. Maxwell, dear; she often speaks in that way to me, when she don't mean anything."

"Mind her! No and yes: she will not worry me; but I shall be glad to have some one to make me remember to be neat at all times. Where's Harty?" said Rosa.

"He's getting ready to go to the woods: he wants you to go with him."

"With all my heart," answered Rosa. "Are we to go now?"

"Yes, as soon as we can put on our bonnets," said Lucy, as she went to her room, to get her things. She put on a pair of thin slippers, although she knew they were to cross a damp meadow, for she could not make up her mind to wear the thick boots that were so much more suitable. Lucy had certain articles of dress which it gave her great pleasure to wear, and these shoes were among the favourites. Many a cold and sore-throat they had cost her, but her vanity was not overcome even by such consequences.

Hand in hand the three children walked merrily along, chatting as pleasantly as if they had not been parted for years.

Rosa and Harty declared that they liked to step on the soft meadow, that it was like a rich carpet that yielded to their feet. Their shoes were so thick that they did not feel the dampness, and they had no idea how uncomfortable Lucy was, in her thin slippers, thoroughly soaked with the moisture. They soon entered the woods, where the tall trees grew so close together that they almost shut out the pleasant sunlight. Here Rosa found so much to admire that she was constantly exclaiming with delight. She had not lived in the country since her childhood, and there was a charm in everything that met her eyes. Sometimes she was struck with new beauties, and sometimes she was reminded of by-gone days.

"Do you remember, Harty," she said, "how we came here together, when you were a little bit of a boy, and made a house under that tree for my doll to lie in? And have you forgotten, when we where gathering chestnuts just here, and I found I had lost my shawl, and how we hunted, and found it at last hanging on the fence by the meadow?"

Harty remembered these and many other occasions when he had enjoyed rambles with his sister; and they continued calling the past to mind, until poor Lucy felt quite sad that she knew nothing of what caused them so much pleasure. She grew silent, and at last withdrew her hand from Rosa, as she thought, "Yes, it will be as Julia Staples said, Harty and Rosa will go together, and not care for me."

The sun was just setting when they drew near home on their return. They had taken a long walk, but Lucy had not recovered her spirits, although Rosa, perceiving that she was not happy, had done all in her power to amuse her. Lucy felt half inclined to laugh and enjoy herself occasionally, but then the wicked, jealous thought would come up in her mind, and she grew sober again, and coldly answered her sister's cheerful remarks.

They had walked through the woods quite round to the back of the house, and were almost to the pleasant orchard, when they came to a wide brook, which they must cross to reach the by-path that led to the house. A single plank was placed across the stream. Harty ran gaily over, and went up the hill on the other side without looking behind him.

"Let me lead you over," said Rosa, kindly offering her hand to her little sister.

"I had rather go by myself," answered Lucy, sullenly, and placed her foot on the plank. She walked tremblingly on until she was half over, then the plank shook a little, and she grew frightened, swayed from side to side, lost her balance, and fell into the brook.

Lucy's shriek attracted the attention of Harty, who was by this time some distance up the hill, and he hastened towards her; but she had scarcely sunk in the water before Rosa had leaped from the bank and caught her in her arms.

The stream was rapid, and the fearless girl could hardly have kept her footing had she not caught hold of the plank above with one hand, while with the other she carried the half-fainting Lucy.

They reached the opposite side in safety, and Harty was there to assist them in climbing the bank. Great tears stood in his eyes, not from fright for Lucy, but from admiration of Rosa's courage.

"You are a sister worth having!" were his first words. "How I wish you were a boy!"

Poor Lucy, what pain these words gave her! Although she had been in such danger, Harty only thought of Rosa!

The true-hearted sister, meanwhile, was lifting her thoughts in thankfulness to Him who had enabled her to save the life of the child.

Lucy was too weak to walk home, and Rosa and Harty formed a lady-chair with their arms, and carried her safely up the hill, Rosa laughing at their ridiculous appearance in their wet clothing, for she had plunged into the stream up to her neck.

"Here we are! all safe and sound!" shouted Harty, as Mrs. Maxwell came out to meet the strange-looking party.

"A pretty-looking set you are! Do not come into the house in that condition!" was Mrs. Maxwell's reply. "Pray where have you been?" she continued: "I wonder if we are to have such doings all the time."

Rosa gently but firmly replied, that Lucy had been in great danger, and she thought she ought to be undressed immediately, and placed in a warm bed.

There was something in Rosa's quiet, dignified manner that awed Mrs. Maxwell: she came forward and took Lucy from their arms without another word, while Rosa hastened to her room to put herself in order to wait upon her sister. In a few moments she was neatly dressed, and standing by Lucy's bedside.

Dr. Vale had returned, and having heard from Harty an account of the matter, was soon with his little daughter. He ordered a warm draught to be administered, and said he did not think she needed any other medicine, as she seemed not to be really injured, only much agitated by the fright.

He kissed the little girl tenderly as he thought how near he had been to losing his pet, and greatly praised Rosa's promptness and courage in saving her from the death with which she was threatened.

Lucy could not thank her sister, for she felt guilty, as she remembered the unkind, suspicious thoughts that were in her mind when the accident happened. She shuddered at the idea that she might have died while her spirit was so unfit to go into the presence of the holy God. She felt that she had been very wicked, and she could not believe that God would pardon her.

"I know I shall be very ill," she said to herself, "because I was so naughty, and perhaps I shall die, and then nobody would care, and Harty and Rosa would be just as happy."

This last thought checked her half-formed resolution to tell her sister of her wrong feelings; and she turned away from the kind face that was bending down to her, and said, "I wish you would go away, I had rather be alone."

Rosa did go, but only to the door of her own room that was opposite: there she placed her chair, that she might be near, if Lucy should be lonely or want anything, little thinking what was in her sister's heart.

Lucy lay very still all the evening. Rosa thought she was sleeping, and did not disturb her. During those long, dark hours, Rosa was not sad. She had many pleasant thoughts. She liked to be alone, sometimes, for then she could more fully realize that God was with her.

Nine o'clock came, yet Rosa did not like to leave her sister: often during the evening she had stolen to her side to see if she were still sleeping. Once she stooped and kissed her; then Lucy longed to throw her arms around the neck of the kind watcher, and say that she had not been asleep; but something kept her silent.

At ten, the doctor came in. Rosa stole softly down stairs and told him how quiet the little girl had been during the evening. "But, dear father," she said, "I do not like to leave her alone to-night. May I not lay her in my bed, where I shall be sure to know if she wakes, and wants anything?"

"Certainly, dear," was the father's reply, "and I will carry her myself, carefully, that she may not wake. She is too heavy for you to lift, though you did take her so nobly through the water, my darling."

The doctor took the little girl gently in his arms; she did not seem to be awake, but oh! how guilty she felt all the time, to think that she had cherished harsh feelings towards one who wished to be so kind to her; and ashamed she felt that she was even then deceiving; but she had not the courage to open her eyes and say that it was all pretence. Rosa covered her very carefully, and placed her head comfortably on the pillow, and then began to move about noiselessly, preparing for the night.

Lucy was just closing her eyes, thinking her bed-fellow was about to lie down beside her, when Rosa threw her wrapper round her, and taking her small Bible, sat down to read. She did not once raise her eyes or move, while she was reading, yet Lucy could see that her expression changed from time to time, as if she was very much interested. There was a sweet peacefulness on her countenance as she closed the book, and Lucy resolved to open at the mark the next morning, that she might read herself what had had so pleasant an effect.

She then looked up and saw that Rosa was kneeling, with her eyes raised, and praying earnestly in a low voice. Lucy was almost startled, Rosa seemed so really to be speaking to some one, and she involuntarily looked about to see if there were any one in the room.

She had been so long accustomed to merely prayers herself, that she had almost forgotten that prayer is always speaking to God.

By degrees she rose in the bed and leaned eagerly forward to catch the words, which were scarcely audible as she lay on the pillow.

She heard her sister earnestly ask pardon for the sins she had just been confessing, while she thanked her Heavenly Father with the confidence of a child for His free forgiveness; and then she prayed, oh, how earnestly! that God would enable her to watch over her brother and sister, and lead them to the dear Saviour, the only source of real happiness, and for whose sake she knew all her petitions would be granted. Before she rose, she begged to be enabled to remember that the Saviour was beside her, through the dark night to preserve her from all harm.

As Rosa finished her prayer, Lucy sank down in the bed, overcome with awe. God was really in the room; Rosa had spoken to Him, and seemed to know that He had heard her. What must His pure eye have seen in her own heart! how much that was wrong! Could He forgive? In a few moments the light was extinguished, and Rosa was at her sister's side. She lay very still at first, that she might not waken the sleeper, but very soon a little hand was laid in hers, and Lucy gently whispered, "Dear Rosa, do you really think the Saviour is near us?"

Rosa was startled to find her companion awake; but she took the little hand instantly, and said, "Yes, dear Lucy, He is with us always."

"Doesn't it make you afraid," said Lucy, "to think so?"

"Afraid to think He is near us, dearest! Why, He is our best friend! Do not you love Him, Lucy?"

Lucy began to sob, and said, at last, that it always frightened her to think about such things, and she never did, unless something reminded her that she must die.

"My dear little sister," said Rosa, "God loves you: you need not be afraid of Him, if you really wish to please Him."

"But I can't please Him, I can't do right," sobbed Lucy.

"I know you cannot," Rosa replied, "but He will forgive you for Jesus' sake, and help you, if you ask Him."

"But I forget all about it," said Lucy.

"It is very hard to remember at first, that God is always with you, and you are trying to be His child. I know, dear Lucy, that you must wish to love and serve the kind Heavenly Father who has done so much for you: begin to-night; ask Him to make you His child, and to take care of you."

Lucy made no answer, but in silence she did as her sister had advised, and God who seeth all hearts received and answered her simple petition.

The few words that Rosa had said, dwelt in her mind. "God loves you," she thought, again and again, as she lay in her quiet bed; and when her eyes closed in sleep, it was with the remembrance that the God who loved her was near to watch over her.

CHAPTER VII
SUNDAY MORNING

Sunday morning came, and the sun was fairly risen before either of the little girls was awake. Rosa was the first to open her eyes: she would willingly have taken another nap, but the first stanza of a morning hymn occurred to her mind, and she remembered her resolution to overcome her laziness.

As she repeated—

> "Awake, my soul, and with the sun
> Thy daily course of duty run,
> Shake off dull sloth, and early rise
> To pay thy morning sacrifice,"

she got up very carefully that she might not rouse her sister. "I will let the child sleep a little longer," she said to herself, "for she is so pale, I don't believe she is quite well."

It was a beautiful morning: the fields and orchards were bright with the sunshine, and the birds seemed singing even more happily than usual. As soon as Rosa had dressed herself, and finished her usual devotions, she went down stairs to enjoy the fresh air. As she walked in the garden, the conversation she had had with Lucy the evening before passed through her mind. What her uncle had said to her about being useful to her own family seemed about to be realized. "Poor little Lucy," she thought: "may God help me to lead the dear child in the right path."

Harty heard Rosa's footsteps in the garden, and was soon at her side. "Here, brother, is something for your museum," was her greeting, and she pointed to a chrysalis which hung on a low rose-twig by the path. "Is it not beautiful? Just look at the silver spots!"

"It is a capital specimen," answered Harty, as he carefully broke the little branch to which it was fastened: "I wonder what kind of a butterfly it will be. Rosa!" he added, "I did not think you would like such things as these."

"Not like the beautiful things God has made!" exclaimed Rosa. "Why, I love to look at every little object in nature, and think that our Heavenly Father planned it and made it so perfect. It seems easy to believe that He notices all our little joys and troubles, when wo see that even the smallest insect is made with such care."

As Rosa spoke, her eyes sparkled and she looked around her, as if every object which was in sight was a proof to her of the love of the kind Creator. Harty made no answer, but looked thoughtfully at the chrysalis as they entered the house together.

The breakfast-bell was ringing, and they met Lucy in the hall. She glanced slyly towards her sister, remembering the conversation of the evening before. Rosa kissed her cordially, and, hand in hand, they went to the table.

"Perhaps Miss Rosa had bettor pour out coffee," said Mrs. Maxwell stiffly to the doctor, as the children came in.

"Would you like it, Rosa?" asked her father.

Rosa saw that Mrs. Maxwell looked displeased, and, in a moment, it passed through her mind, that perhaps she would not like to give up the place she had held so long to one so young as herself, and she quickly said,—

"May I put that off a little longer, father? I am afraid I could not suit you as well as Mrs. Maxwell does; she has made tea for you a great while."

"A long time, dear child," said the doctor; and his thoughts went back to the days when his delicate wife sat opposite him, her sweet face growing paler each morning, until at last her weak hands could no longer do their office, and Mrs. Maxwell took her place.

Rosa knew of what her father must be thinking, and she did not speak for several minutes. At length she said, "Is old Mr. Packard any better to-day, father?"

"I have not seen him yet," was the reply. "I shall have to make a round of visits this morning," continued the doctor, "so I shall not have the pleasure of taking my tall daughter to church to-day: I leave that to Harty."

Harty looked very proud at the idea of waiting on his sister. Little Lucy listened in vain to hear something said about her forming one of the party. She resolved, at least, to get ready, and perhaps no one would object to her going.

When they rose from the breakfast-table, Rosa went to her room, thinking she should have a quiet hour to herself before it was time to prepare for church; but Lucy and Harty followed her. The rules had been very strict at Mr. Gillette's: the young ladies seldom, visited each other in their bed-rooms, and then never entered without knocking.

The freedom with which her sister went in and out of her apartment was already an annoyance to Rosa, and her first impulse was to send them away, that she might read her Bible alone, as she had intended. Then her confirmation vow came to her remembrance. She had promised "to love her neighbour as herself, to do unto others as she would they should do unto her." Would she like to be sent away from a person she loved? and was it not a part of her duty to make those around her happy? Her first impulse was conquered, and she turned cheerfully to the children, who felt uncomfortable for a moment, they hardly knew why, and said, "Come, let us sit here by the window; I am going to read, and you shall listen to me, if you please."

They looked delighted. Lucy dropped upon a low footstool by her sister's side, and Harty stood watching eagerly to see what was to be the chosen book. He seemed disappointed when Rosa took up her little Bible, and shook his head when she asked him if he would not take the vacant chair beside her.

She began to read in the fifth chapter of Mark, "And, behold, there cometh one of the rulers of the synagogue, Jairus by name; and when he saw Him [Jesus], he fell at His feet, and besought Him greatly, saying, My little daughter lieth at the point of death: I pray thee, come and lay thy hands on her, that she may be healed; and she shall live."

Rosa had taken great pains to learn to read properly and pleasantly, for her uncle had told her that to be an agreeable reader was one way of being useful. Now her voice was sweet and natural, and she seemed herself so interested, that Lucy caught her spirit even before the "little daughter" was mentioned; but at these words her attention was fixed, and she listened eagerly to hear what was to follow.

Harty, meanwhile, stood rolling the corner of the neat white curtain in his hands, which were not particularly clean, and looking undecidedly about him. When Rosa finished the sentence, he hurried from the room, saying, "I'm going to see my chickens."

She glanced at the soiled curtain and then at Harty as he closed the door: for a moment she looked fretted, but it was only a moment; a sweet smile took the place of the half-formed frown, and she went on with the reading.

Lucy had heard the story before of the raising of the ruler's daughter, but now it seemed quite new to her, and her eyes were bright with wonder and pleasure, as her sister closed the book.

"Rosa," she said, "I should like to have been that little girl!"

"Why?" said Rosa,

"Because—because," answered Lucy—"because she must have been so glad to be alive again. I wonder what she said when they told her all that had happened."

"I hope she thanked the land Saviour, and learned to love Him very dearly."

"How sorry she must have been that the Saviour could not stay and live at her home, and take care of her always," said Lucy.

"Lucy," said Rosa, "the same thing may happen to you as to that little girl; but after Christ has said to you, Arise, you may live with Him always."

Lucy looked half-frightened, and answered, "I don't understand you. I should have to die first;" and she shuddered at the thought.

"No; you may have Christ with you always, without dying, but you cannot see Him. He will take care of you, and you can speak to Him, and He will do what you ask Him. If you remember that He loves you and is ever at your side, when you come to die it will seem like opening your eyes to see the kind Friend who has been so long with you."

Lucy's eyes filled with tears, and in her heart she wished that she loved the Saviour as Rosa did. "I will try and remember that He is with me," she said to herself; and for the first time the idea was pleasant to her. Before she had only thought of God as seeing her when she was doing wrong, and it had always been a very painful thought to her.

Many minutes had passed when Lucy started up, saying, "There goes the church bell; it is time to get ready."

Rosa and Lucy were quite ready, when Harty came running into the room, his hair in its usual tumbled state, and his coat dusty and torn. "Oh! I have had such a chase," he said: "one of my 'bantys' got out, and I had to jump over the fence and chase him all over the orchard before I could catch him. And see here, where I tore my coat putting him back in the coop. Why! you are all ready: is it church-time?"

"Yes, indeed," answered Lucy; "and I hate to be late, people all look at you so."

"I hate to be late, too," said Harty; "I do like to watch the people come in."

"Harty! Harty!" interrupted Rosa; "don't talk so. Make haste and get ready."

"Never mind me," said Harty; "you walk on, and I can catch up with you: it won't take me but a minute to change my coat—these trowsers will do."

"But, Harty, you will have to brush your hair and your shoes, and wash yourself. It would not be respectful to the place where you are going to enter in such a plight."

"Pshaw!" said Harty, angrily; "I will not go at all; you can find your way, with little Lucy to open the door for you."

Rosa was tempted to leave him, for she, too, disliked to be late at church, but not for either of the reasons that had been mentioned. She liked to be in her seat before the service commenced, that she might have time to collect her thoughts, and be ready to join with the congregation in the solemn worship of God.

"My brother ought not to stay at home," she thought: "it will be better to wait for him, even if we are late." "Come, Harty," said she, encouragingly, "we will help you, and you will soon be ready."

Lucy was dispatched to the kitchen for the shoes that had been cleaned, for Harty's cap, pocket-hankerchief, another clean collar, &c.; in short, she had so many things to run for, that she stopped on the landing, so weary that she was glad to take breath. There Mrs. Maxwell met her, and said, "Take off those things, Lucy Vale; you ought not to think of going to church after the wetting you got yesterday. Your father didn't say you might go; I noticed it this morning."

"But I am quite well," pleaded Lucy. "I think he would let me go, if he were at home."

"But he is not at home. At noon you can ask him. Go now and undress as fast as you can." Without another word Mrs. Maxwell passed down stairs.

Lucy dropped down upon the lowest stop, and began to cry bitterly.

"Ready at last!" shouted Harty: "now Lucy, my Prayer Book."

But no Lucy came. Rosa and Harty came towards her, and wore astonished to see her face wot with tears.

"What is the matter?" asked Rosa: "have you hurt yourself?"

"No!" sobbed Lucy; "but Mrs. Maxwell says I must not go to church."

"Pooh! is that all?" said Harty; "why, you are not always so fond of church-going!"

This was true, for Lucy often stayed away from church when Mrs. Maxwell did not oblige her to go; but on this particular morning she wanted to go with her sister, whom she was beginning to love very dearly.

"But why mustn't you go?" asked Rosa.

"Because I got in the water yesterday, and Mrs. Maxwell says I am not well."

"Never mind, dear," said Rosa, "perhaps father will let you go out this afternoon. Don't cry any more; we shall not be gone long. Good-bye."

Harty was rather glad that Lucy could not go; he never liked to take Lucy anywhere with him. Perhaps he thought it made him appear more like a mere boy to have his little sister by his side, or that she was not fit to associate with so wise a gentleman as himself.

If his sister Rosa had felt as ungenerously and unkindly to those younger than herself, she would have at least laughingly refused the arm which he offered her as they went down the walk. But she took the arm, although she had to stoop a little in doing so, and talked with her brother as if he really were the man he was trying to appear.

As Harty was thus honoured, he looked back triumphantly at poor Lucy, who was still watching them. A pang of envy shot through the heart of the little girl. Julia Staples's evil words came to her mind; the bad seed was springing up. "Rosa and Harty will always be together; they won't care for me," she thought. But good seed had been sown by Rosa, and it, too, now sprang up. "God loves me," thought the little girl; "if I try to please Him I shall be happy."

She rose and wont into her own pretty room: there she put everything carefully in its proper place, and felt a new pleasure in doing so; for it was her duty.

CHAPTER VIII
STAYING AT HOME

The house was very still, and as Lucy moved about she was half startled at the sound of her own footsteps. She went into her sister's room to sit, for she fancied that it was more pleasant than her own; and then all Rosa's books were there; perhaps she might like to look at some of them.

The Bible was on the table; she took it up. "Rosa, from her Uncle Gillette," was written on the blank leaf; and before it were several sentences. They were as follows:—"Remember when you open this book, that God is with you, that He is speaking to you. Remember to ask God to bless to you what you read. When you close the book, think over what you have been reading, and take the first opportunity to practise it."

As Lucy read the first sentence, a fooling of awe stole over her; and she almost trembled to think how often she had carelessly opened the word of God, and hurried over its sacred pages. Now she reverently turned to the place where her sister had left the mark the evening before. The story of the storm on the sea of Galilee caught her eye: as she read it she felt sure that it must have been that sweet narrative which had so fixed Rosa's attention when she watched her.

Lucy repeated, again and again, the words of the blessed Saviour, "Why are ye so fearful, O ye of little faith?" They seemed addressed to her by the kind Friend who stilled the tempest, and who, Rosa had said, would be ever with her to take care of her, if she would love Him and strive to be truly His child. "I will, I will love Him, and try to please Him," she said, half-aloud. "I should never be afraid, if I were sure He would watch over me."

She took up the Prayer Book, and read the verses with which the Morning Service commences. Some of them she did not quite understand; but when she came to "I will arise, and go to my father, and will say unto him, Father, I have sinned against heaven, and before thee, and am no more worthy to be called thy son," she was reminded of the day when her sister had read to her the sweet parable from which those words are taken, and how she had said that one purpose of the parable was to show how willing God is to receive all those who really come to Him. Again her purpose strengthened to be His child, who could so freely forgive.

Lucy had been over the same Service almost every Sunday since she had been able to read, and could now find all the places without assistance, but she had hardly noticed many parts of it, and to some she had listened, while they were repeated by others, as if she had no part in the matter. Now the exhortation, "Dearly beloved brethren, the Scripture moveth us in sundry places," seemed so direct and simple, that she wondered she could ever have heard it without feeling for how important a purpose she had come into the house of God.

With a strange feeling of solemnity, she knelt down and began to repeat the Confession aloud. The words were so simple and natural, and so true, that she seemed rather to be speaking what had long been in her heart, than repeating what had been spoken by many voices around her from Sunday to Sunday, while she thoughtlessly glanced on the page, or let her mind wander to other things. As she said, "We have done those things that we ought not to have done," little faults she had committed, acts known only to herself, came thronging on her memory. Among these painful recollections was the falsehood she had told about the light the morning after the thunderstorm. The whole fearful scene of that night came back to her: again she seemed standing, trembling and alone, in the passage, while the incessant lightning appeared to threaten her with instant death. So long she dwelt on these circumstances, that she quite forgot she was on her knees, speaking to the mighty God of heaven. Suddenly it flashed upon her, and she started up, as if she feared He would immediately punish her for seeming to be praying, while her thoughts were far away. Lucy had begun to realize that prayer is something more than merely repeating a form of words.

The little girl had hardly risen from her knees before there was a ring at the door. She set off immediately to save Betsy the trouble of coming up stairs, for the poor old woman suffered much from rheumatism, and Lucy knew it gave her great pain to move about. "I will go, Betsy," she called, as she passed the stairway.

A ragged Irishman was standing at the door. Lucy was almost afraid to turn the key, lest he should lay hold of her with his hard, rough hands: she felt inclined to call out to him to go away, as the doctor was not at home; but she thought of the misery that giving way to her fear of Mrs. Tappan's dog had cost her, and her father's reproof, and she resolved that no poor sufferer should go uncared-for because she was afraid to speak to a man in ragged clothes.

She threw the door wide open, and was quite relieved when the Irishman took off his hat, and asked her very respectfully, "Is the doctor in?"

"He is not," answered Lucy, promptly: "where shall I tell him to call?"

"Sure and it's jist down the lane, forninst Bridget O'Brady's: he can't miss it, for isn't it the poorest bit of roof in the place? and tell him to come quick, if you plase, miss."

The man turned to go away, but Lucy called after him, not at all satisfied that the direction would be sufficient. "What is your name?" she asked; "I want to put it down on the slate for my father."

"It's Owen M'Grath, plase you; and don't be afther stopping me, for who will be minding the baby, and the mother so sick, while I am jist talking here?" So saying, he hurried from the door.

Lucy had very little idea how the name was to be spelt, but she put it down as well as she could, the direction and all, and looked at it quite proudly when it was done. It was neatly written, but oh, the spelling!

"Who was that, Miss Lucy?" called Betsy.

"An Irishman with a queer name: he says he lives by Bridget O'Brady's," was the reply.

"Oh! dreadful!" shouted Betsy. "Why, Miss Lucy, they've got the small-pox in all them dirty little houses; you've ketched it for certain. Go, take off every rag of clothes you've got on, and throw them into the tub there in the yard: I don't know who'll wash 'em. I am sure I should not want to touch 'em with a broomstick."

Poor Lucy, pale and trembling, ran up stairs and did as Betsy had advised. Even in the midst of her fright she could not help thinking that she was glad it was her calico, not the favourite silk, that she happened to have on, since she must thrust it into the water, to lie there till some one should dare to remove it.

The happy birds were still singing about the pretty cottage, and the trees were waving in the sunshine, but Lucy did not see them; her hands were pressed tightly over her eyes, and she rocked to and fro, thinking of all the horrible stories she had heard about the disease which Betsy said she had "ketched for certain."

"I shall be very ill," she thought, "and who will dare to nurse me? Perhaps I shall die; and if I get well, my face will be all marked, so that nobody will like to look at me. I wonder if Rosa would be afraid to sit by my bed, if nobody else would stay with me. I should hate to see her face all pitted. How badly I should feel if she should take the small-pox from me. Perhaps I shall give it to her if I see her now." At this last thought, Lucy ran into her own little room. There she sat sobbing until church was out. She forgot that there was a Friend with her, in that quiet room, who could have given her comfort, if she had called on Him in her trouble.

CHAPTER IX
THE KING AND HIS WEAPONS

Rosa and Harty were scarcely out of the church door before he began, "Oh! Rosa, did you see how grand Madam Maxwell looked, when she moved for you to take the end of the pew? It was as much as to say, 'I suppose, little miss, you think you ought to sit here, but you are very presuming.' I would have taken it if I had been in your place. It made me mad to see her settle herself so satisfied, when you refused."

"Fie, Harty!" answered Rosa; "Mrs. Maxwell is a great deal older than I am, and it is far more suitable that she should have the most comfortable seat. I should be sorry if my coming home interfered with her in any way. She has been most faithful in taking charge of the house since—since—" since our dear mother died, Rosa would have added, but her eyes filled and her voice failed her. The familiar scene in the church had brought her lost mother freshly before her, and she well remembered when they last trod that same path together.

After a few moments she recovered herself, and said, "When I last passed this spot, Harty, our dear mother was with me. She had been talking very sweetly to me, as we walked, of the blessing we had in being able to go out that pleasant morning, and worship God with His people, while so many poor invalids must remain at home, and even dear father could not be with us. Just here, I asked her a question which had long been in my mind. I had always noticed that as soon as she entered the pew, she knelt down for a few minutes. I wondered what that was for, as I could not find anything about it in the Prayer Book. 'Mother,' said I, 'what do you say when you kneel down before church begins?' 'I make a short prayer,' she answered, 'that I may remember that I am in God's house, and that He will teach me to worship Him aright. Many people,' she continued, 'who come early to church, quite forget that they are in the house of God as much before the service begins as afterwards, and spend the time until the clergyman comes in, in looking about and observing their neighbours, until their minds are quite unfit to join in any solemn duty. I think the habit of asking the blessing of God on the prayers you are about to offer, and the truths you are about to hear, is a great help in reminding you immediately that you are with the Lord in His holy temple.' 'Won't you teach me a little prayer to say, that I may do as you do?' I asked. 'Yes, darling,' she answered, with one of her sweet, loving smiles; and as we walked by this hedge, which was just planted then, she taught me these words, which I have said, many, many times since our dear mother was taken by her Heavenly Father to a better world: —

"'Lord, make me remember that I am in Thy house. Keep me from dullness and wandering thoughts. Hear my prayers to-day, and bless to my soul the truths I shall hear, for Jesus Christ's sake. Amen.'"

Harty listened with interest to every word that Rosa tittered: he often wanted to hear some one talk of his mother, but it was too sad a subject for his father to speak freely upon, and Lucy could hardly remember her.

Rosa gladly perceived that he was interested, and added, "I will write out the little prayer for you, Harty; I know you will like to keep it, and use it, for our dear mother's sake."

Harty looked embarrassed, but he did not refuse his sister's offer. She immediately changed the subject by saying, "Poor little Lucy will be glad to see us by this time. I hope she can go out this afternoon. I like to have her with us."

Harty wondered that Rosa should wish for the society of such a child as Lucy; but his respect for her involuntarily rose when he found that Rosa spoke affectionately of her.

As they drew near the house, they caught a glimpse of Lucy looking sorrowfully from her window. She did not run to meet them, as they expected, but old Betsy came out saying, "Oh! only think of it! Miss Lucy has got the small-pox, I know she has. There's been a man here that must have it, for he lives down by Bridget O'Brady's, where they are dirty enough to make them all ill."

Rosa was startled for a moment, but she answered calmly, "But Lucy has been vaccinated, Betsy; she would not take the small-pox even if the man really had it."

"I don't believe nothin' at all in *vaxnation*," said Betsy; "it don't stand to reason. I telled Miss Lucy she'd ketched the small-pox, and I believe she has."

"Poor child!" said Rosa; and she ran hastily up stairs. Harty did not follow, for although he laughed at Lucy's timidity, he was a bit of a coward about some things himself; and old Betsy's words had alarmed him not a little.

"Let me in, Lucy," said Rosa's sweet voice entreatingly; "I could not take the small-pox if you had it."

Lucy gladly unfastened the door. Rosa took the trembling girl in her lap. For a few moments Lucy sobbed violently, and not a word was spoken; at length Rosa said, tenderly, "Dear Lucy, there is no danger of what you dread so much. Here, let me look at those little arms: there is the scar where you wore vaccinated when you were a baby, that you might never take the small-pox. Your kind father took good care that his little Lucy should not have her smooth face all pitted."

"Can't I have it?" asked Lucy, the tears still in her eyes.

"No! certainly not!" was the reply.

"But, dearest," continued Rosa, "you may be exposed to other diseases quite as dangerous. I wish you could learn to trust the Heavenly Father, who loves you more dearly even than our own papa; then you would not be afraid of anything. Shall I tell you what I heard uncle Gillette saying to one of the little girls at school, who was afraid of lightning."

"Oh! do," said Lucy; "I am so frightened when it thunders."

Lucy nestled closer in her sister's lap, and Rosa began.

"There was once a mighty king who was so terrible in war that all his enemies were afraid of him; the very sound of his name made them tremble. His arm was so strong that the horse and its rider would sink under one blow of his battle-axe; and when he struck with his sharp sword, his enemies fell dead at his feet. This mighty king had a little fair-haired daughter, who watched him as he prepared for the battle. She saw him put on his helmet, and laughed as the plumes nodded above his brow. She saw the stately battle-axe brought forth; she saw him take his keen sword in his hand; he tried its edge, then waved it about his head in the sunlight. She laughed as it glanced sparkling through the air; and even while it was upheld she ran towards her father to take a parting kiss. Why was not the little child afraid of the mighty king with the fierce weapons? Because he was her father; she knew that he loved her, loved her as his own life. She knew that those dangerous weapons would never be used against her unless to save her from worse peril. Do you understand what uncle Gillette meant by this story?"

"Not exactly," said Lucy; "won't you tell me?"

"He meant," said Rosa, "that God is like that mighty king. Sickness, lightning, danger, trial, death, are all His weapons; but we need not fear them if we are truly His children. When the sharp lightning flashes in the sky, we can look calmly at its beauty, for it is in our Father's hand. Sickness may be around us, but our Father can keep us safe. Death may come, but it will only be to send us to our Father's arms."

"But I am not His child," half sobbed Lucy.

"His child you are, my dear little sister: His loving, obedient child, I hope you will be."

At this moment the dinner-bell rang. Rosa waited till Lucy could wash away the traces of her tears and smooth her hair, and then they went down stairs together. Mrs. Maxwell looked up with a smile as Rosa came in; her thoughtful deference was beginning to have its effect.

"Hurrah! for the small-pox!" shouted Harty, as Lucy came in. He had heard from his father that the danger was imaginary, and, forgetting his own fears, he quite despised Lucy for her fright.

"Come here, my little patient," said the doctor to the blushing child. "I don't wonder my pet was frightened: old Betsy ought to be ashamed for being so foolish. Poor Owen M'Grath could injure no one; his sorrow is his worst disease. You see I made out the name in your spelling, and I am obliged to my little girl for trying to write the message so exactly. Owen had as neat a little home as you could wish to see, but it is a sad, sad place now. His poor wife has long been ill with consumption; she died this noon, and there is no one to take charge of his little baby but his daughter, who is only as old as you are, Lucy."

"Can we not do something for them, father?" asked Rosa.

"How like her mother," thought the doctor. "Yes, dear child," he replied; "I will take you to see them to-morrow."

"May I go too?" asked Harty, eagerly.

The father smiled and nodded his head. "We will not leave little Lucy behind, either," he added, to her great delight; "that is, if she is well enough. My pet looks a little pale yet. You did well, Mrs. Maxwell, not to let her go out this morning."

Mrs. Maxwell gave a glance at Lucy, which made her drop her eyes.

"I shall not be at home to hear your catechism this evening, Lucy," said Mrs. Maxwell, as she left the dinner-table; "I am going to see a sick friend after church, as Miss Rosa can take my place at tea-time."

"Willingly," said Rosa, "and hear the catechism too," she added, internally.

CHAPTER X
THE HAPPY SUNDAY EVENING

Sunday afternoon passed away very rapidly to Lucy. She spent the time while her brother and sister were at church in reading a little book which Rosa had lent her.

As the children sat together in the twilight, after tea, Rosa said to Lucy, "We used to call you baby and pet at first: do you know when we began to call you Lucy?"

"Not till I was two months old, I've heard father say."

"Yes; I well remember the morning that you took your new name," continued Rosa. "It was a bright day in June. Dear mamma was so kind and cheerful then. I can see her now as she came in to breakfast, so slender and pale, and yet with such a calm, happy look on her face.

"'You must call the baby Lucy after to-day,' she said to me, as I kissed her that morning.

"'And why, dear mother?' I asked.

"'Because she is to be baptized to-day, and take Lucy for her Christian name,' answered our mother.

"'But why is the baby to be baptized?' I childishly asked. She took no notice of my question then; but after breakfast was over, she called me to her side, and said, 'Shall I tell my little girl a story?'

"'Oh, do!' I answered, and she began.

"'There was once a little child who lived in a very small cottage, with a scanty grass plat before it. This child had a pet lamb, of which she was very fond. She loved it so dearly that she often sat on the door-step and anxiously thought how she should ever be able to keep it from harm as it grew older, and would be tempted to run away from the cottage, around which there was not even a light paling. Then winter must come, and how would the poor little lamb be protected from the storm?

"'These thoughts were one day in the child's mind, when an old traveller came to the cottage door, and said to her, "I have a message to you, dear child, from the shepherd who feeds his flock on yonder green hill. He has noticed you and your little lamb, and he wants to be a friend to you. He knows that you will never be able to keep your pet from harm, although you love it so tenderly; and he bade me say to you, that he is willing to take your lamb to be one of his flock, to feed in that green pasture and drink from the clear stream that is ever flowing there. It shall be safely gathered to his fold when the storms of winter beat, and shall be guarded from all cruel beasts. You can see it every day, and caress it, though you must never try to lead it away from him. Shall we go together and lead the little lamb to the kind shepherd?"

"'"Yes!" shouted the child, joyfully; and she took the old traveller's hand, and gently led the lamb away by the blue ribbon that was about its neck.

"'It was but a short distance they had to go, yet the traveller found time to tell the child, as they walked together, that if her lamb learned to know the shepherd's voice, and follow him, he would take it some day to a beautiful land, where it could hunger and thirst no more; where there would be no more storms, nor cruel beasts, and where she might meet it and dwell for ever with the kind shepherd and his blessed flock.

"'The child did not see the kind shepherd; but the peaceful sheep, feeding on the delicate food, or lying beside the clear water, were there, and she did not fear to leave her pet among them. Day by day she saw her lamb grow stronger and happier, and more pure and gentle, and she rejoiced that she had placed it among the favoured flock.

"'One day the little child grew dizzy and faint: all things around her seemed fading from her sight, and her dim eyes could only see a strange figure which seemed beckoning her away.

"'Then at her side she heard the voice of the old traveller who had visited her before: "Fear not," said he; "you are going to the beautiful land where the kind shepherd dwells." Then a pang shot through the heart of the child, for she thought of the lamb that she must leave behind her. The traveller guessed her thoughts, and answered, "Your little lamb is in the care of the kind shepherd!" Then the eyes of the child were bright, and she said, "I don't fear for my little lamb: I am happy that I placed him where he will be so tenderly cared for, when I did not know that I so soon must leave him. May he learn to know the kind shepherd's voice, and follow him, that we may meet again in the beautiful land."

"'The cottage was soon all silence: the child no longer went singing from room to room, but she was happy, far away in the blessed land which the kind shepherd prepared for his faithful flock.'"

"'Did the little lamb go to meet her there?' I asked, as dear mamma stopped as if she had finished the story.

"'I cannot tell you, Rosa,' she answered, and fast the tears fell from her eyes. 'By the lamb I mean your little sister, and the kind shepherd is the Saviour, to whom I am to give her to-day. God only knows whether our little Lucy will reach the blessed land.'

"'But you are not going away, mamma, as the child did,' I said, my eyes, too, filling with tears, for I too well understood her meaning.

"'Perhaps not very soon,' she answered, and smiled away her tears."

Lucy was still silent, and Rosa went on, for both Harty and Lucy were earnestly listening.

"When you were carried up the aisle, dear Lucy, all in your white clothing, you seemed to me like the little lamb of which mother had spoken, and I felt that you were being received into the flock of the kind shepherd. You smiled when the water was sprinkled on your forehead, and I was so glad, for that made you seem willing to be placed in His care."

Lucy listened to the story of the child and the lamb; and when she heard its explanation her heart was full, and she inwardly resolved that she would try so to follow the Saviour here, that she might join her mother at last in His blessed land. As Rosa recalled the circumstances of her Baptism, she for the first time realized that it had really happened, that her name had been really given by her "sponsors in Baptism."

"Was I there too?" asked Harty, beginning to be restless, as there was a short pause.

"Yes, indeed! and so eager to see the ceremony that you climbed on to the seat, and leaned forward to look until you fell with a loud noise, just as the baby was being carried out of church. You always were a noisy fellow," said Rosa, as she laid her hand affectionately on her brother's clustered curls.

"Did I cry?" asked Harty.

"No; you thought yourself too much of a man for that, even then; and how fondly, proudly, mamma looked at you, as you closed your little lips and stood up without a sound, though there was a bright red mark on your forehead where you had struck it."

It seemed strange to Harty that he was willing to sit still and listen to a girl; yet he found a pleasure in being with Rosa different from any he had ever felt. He had always been quite indifferent as to what Lucy thought of him, but that Rosa should not be pleased with him was a very unpleasant idea. As a child he had tenderly loved his mother; and when she was taken from him, a blank had been left in his heart which had never been filled. Now half the charm of Rosa's society consisted in her being able to speak of that mother, and revive his now fading remembrance of her.

"Come," said Rosa, "let us say our Catechism together: I will ask the questions, and we will all repeat the answers."

Lucy was delighted at the idea, and readily joined her voice with Rosa's. She found it difficult to keep with her sister in reciting, as Rosa repeated her answers slowly, as if she really meant what she was saying. As she pronounced the words, "a member of Christ, a child of God," she looked meaningly at Lucy; and then it flashed through the little girl's mind, that she was indeed the child of God, as her sister had said; His child, not only because He had made her, but because she had been made His by Baptism; and again she resolved to be His "loving, obedient child."

At first Harty did not join in saying the Catechism; he had for some time given up the practice as a thing only for such children as Lucy; but when he saw that Rosa did not think it beneath her, as they came to the Apostles' Creed his voice mingled with the others. Rosa took no notice of it save that she placed her hand in his, and they went on. In some of the long answers Lucy faltered, and Harty halted entirely; but Rosa smoothly continued until they could again join her. As Harty repeated the once familiar words, he recalled the time when he had learned them from that mother who was now a saint in Paradise. With those familiar words returned the precious lessons of love and holiness which she had spoken, but which he had forgotten amid the sport and recklessness of boyhood.

When they had finished, he was quite softened, and his voice was very gentle as he replied to Rosa's proposal to sing, "Yes, if I know anything you do."

Lucy was fond of music, but she could not sing: she laid her head on her sister's lap, and listened to the simple hymns with a feeling of peace and happiness. Another and another hymn was sung, until, at last, the clock struck nine.

"Nine o'clock," said Harty, "and Lucy not in bed! what would Mrs. Maxwell say to that?"

Lucy had been fast asleep, and was not a little frightened when she heard it was so late. She took a candle immediately, kissed her sister and wished her good night. Oh! what pleasure it gave her when Harty said, "Me, too, if you please," and really looked fondly in her face.

That night she forgot to look for robbers; she was too happy to think of them; but she did not forget the many blessings of the day when she repeated her usual thanksgiving. The same prayers she had often said she used that evening; but they went up from her heart, and were received in heaven for the Redeemer's sake.

CHAPTER XI
JUDY M'GRATH

Often, during school-hours on Monday, the promised visit to Owen M'Grath's came into Lucy's mind, and she longed for four o'clock to come, that she might be at liberty. School was over at last, and with the pleasant consciousness of having done well the duties of the day, Lucy tripped towards home. Julia Staples had tried several times to draw her into a whispered conversation, but she had resisted the temptation; and when Julia offered her an apple, and put her arm in hers, to draw her aside for a confidential chat, Lucy refused the gift and got away as soon as she could with politeness. She had learned that the first step towards doing right, is to keep as much as possible out of the way of temptation; and she knew that Julia's society roused her evil feelings.

"Dear me, how stuck-up somebody is!" said Julia Staples to one of her companions, as Lucy turned away.

Lucy heard the remark, and her face flushed slightly, but she made no reply.

Julia did not offer to accompany Lucy home, but with two of the scholars, who were much like herself, she walked behind the little girl, "making fun of her." Of this Lucy knew nothing. Lightly and rapidly she walked along, not looking behind her, but welcoming each turn in the road that brought her nearer home.

Rosa and Harty were standing at the door to meet her. "I do believe you were kept in," began Harty; "we have been waiting for you this half-hour."

"Come, come! young gentleman," interposed Rosa playfully, "you are in such a hurry to wait on the ladies, that the time seems long to you. It is but five minutes past four."

The teased, fretted expression that was coming over Lucy's face passed away in an instant, and Harty's impatience was changed to a smile.

The children, set off together in high spirits. Even Rosa, although she know she was going to the house of mourning, caught something of their spirit, and chatted cheerfully by the way.

Dr. Vale was just driving up to Owen's door when they arrived.

"That's right! all punctual," said he, as he alighted; and when he looked upon their bright faces, he felt thankful that his little group had been so far spared from sickness and death. The happy young voices were hushed in an instant, as they entered the dark, quiet room, into which the street-door opened. There was but a little furniture, and that of the plainest sort, yet all was neat and tidy. The pale, lifeless form of the mother was stretched upon the bed, and close at its side there nestled a sleeping infant, rosy with health.

The little girl, who was sitting beside them, her head on her hands, jumped up as the strangers came in. She instantly recognised the doctor, and said, in a low voice, "Won't the docther plase to be sated, and the young gintleman and ladies?"

Noiselessly she put forward the chairs, and whispered as she did so, "Whisht! the poor babby has been grievin' so I could not hush him at all, and sorra a bit would he sleep till I laid him there by poor mammy, and then he cuddled up to her cold side and seemed quite contint."

"Poor baby!" said Rosa, the tears in her eyes.

They all drew near to the bed, and looked into the face of the dead. Harty gave one glance and then stepped to the door; he could not bear it; he felt a choking in his throat to which he was quite unaccustomed.

As Rosa and Lucy looked upon the calm, sweet expression of the face, they felt no chill of horror. Death seemed less terrible to Lucy than it had ever done before. "She is happy now?" half questioned she of Rosa.

Rosa looked puzzled, but the doctor replied, "Yes, she is happy. 'I'm going home,' were her last words. She has only gone to be with the Friend whom she has served faithfully through life."

"Did you say mammy was happy?" asked Judy, the little girl who had been acting as nurse.

"Happy with the angels in heaven," was the doctor's reply.

"Then I'd not want her back again, to be sorrying here. Little peace she's had, with that misery in her side, for many a day. Why, the lifting of Larry there, was enough to make her all put to it for an hour. Poor fayther, he can't get along with it all: sorra a bit has he tasted to-day, and he cried fit to break his heart when he went away to work this morning; but he said he must go, for he'd niver a sixpence to pay for the burying."

The poor little girl had been so long alone that it seemed to be quite a relief to her to talk to some one who felt for her.

"You'll be a comfort to him, I know," said Rosa, gently.

"I'll lave nothing untiched that I can turn my hand to," answered Judy, earnestly.

The talking, although it was in a low voice, waked Larry, and he began to moan piteously. He put out his hand, touched the cold face near him, and then drew it quickly away. He half-raised his head, but seeing that it was his mother's cheek that had so startled him, he again put forth his hand and patted her gently until he was again asleep.

"And what will poor Larry do when they lay her in the cold ground?" said little Judy, half crying.

"He will soon be comforted," whispered Rosa: "God will take care of you both. It must have been a long time since your mother has been able to sew," she continued, to divert Judy's mind from her trouble.

"Ach! yes. She has not set a stitch for two months gone; and there's Larry, with sorra a bit of clothes but them he has on, savin' this thrifle of a frock that I've been trying to wash for the burying."

As she said this she put her hand on a little faded calico frock that was hanging near the window.

"I think we can get some clothes for Larry," said Rosa: "may I take this home with me for a pattern?"

Judy looked a little confused, but she answered, "Sartainly, miss."

"Can you sew, Judy?" asked Rosa.

"I never was learnt," was Judy's reply.

"Would you like to have me teach you? If you would, you may come to me every Saturday morning, and I will show you how."

Judy's eyes brightened, and she was going to accept the offer very gladly, when she thought of Larry, and changed her mind.

"I can't lave Larry; there's nobody but me to mind him now."

"You may bring him with you; I know Lucy here will take care of him," said Rosa.

"Oh yes, I will, if he won't be afraid to stay with me," said Lucy.

Before they left the house it was agreed that Judy should come the next Saturday morning for her first lesson in sewing, if her father did not object.

Dr. Vale, who had been standing without the door with Harty, met the girls as they came out. He stepped back when Judy was alone, and placed some money in her hand, telling her to give it to her father, and say to him, that his children should not want for a friend while Dr. Vale was in the neighbourhood.

Judy curtseyed, and spoke her thanks as well as she was able, but they were not heard, for the doctor hurried away, and in a few moments had driven from the door.

Very little was said on the way home. As they passed an old house, with a rough, high fence about it, Harty told his sisters that this was where the people had been sick with small-pox.

Lucy clasped Rosa's hand a little closer, and they both stopped more rapidly.

"Father says nobody need be afraid, for they have all got well, and nobody took it from them," said Harty.

Notwithstanding this assurance, all the party felt more easy when the house with the high fence was out of sight.

"Let us stop here and buy the cloth for Larry's frocks," said Rosa, as they reached the village shop.

While Rosa was looking at some cheap woollen cloth, Harty was fumbling in his pockets. He drew out some marbles, an old knife, a peg-top, and some bits of string, and at last he found what he was seeking—a half-crown, with which he had intended to buy some new fishing-tackle. He gave one longing look at the money, and then handed it to Rosa, saying, "Take that for the cloth."

"Yes," said she, very quietly; but a bright, loving smile was on her face, and Harty felt, happy, although he was blushing as if he had been in mischief. Like many boys, Harty seemed to feel more ashamed when he did right than when he did wrong.

When the children were gathered round the table in the evening, Rosa brought out the old dress, and was just putting the scissors to it when Mrs. Maxwell exclaimed, "What are you doing, child? are you going to cut that dress to pieces?"

"I was going to rip it for a pattern," answered Rosa, mildly.

"I suppose you think I could not cut out a frock nice enough for a little Paddy boy," said Mrs. Maxwell.

"Oh no, I did not think that!" Rosa replied, smiling; "I should be very glad to have you help us."

Mrs. Maxwell took the scissors, and the frocks were soon cut out, much to Rosa's relief, for although she had resolved to do it, it was her first attempt at dressmaking, and she was afraid that she should only spoil the cloth.

Then the sewing commenced, and the needles flew so fast that there was little time for talking. Lucy was allowed to make the skirt, and she sewed it as carefully as if it had been an apron for her doll, and that was very nicely. Mrs. Maxwell put on her spectacles and began to sew too, much to Rosa's surprise; and once she offered to turn the hem for Lucy, when she saw that she was troubled. It seemed as if the work they were doing put them all in a good humour, for every face was bright and happy. Even Harty felt as if he had something to do in the business, and instead of fidgeting about as usual, annoying everybody, he sat very still for some time, doing no harm, but breaking off thread from the ball and tying it into knots. At last he said, "Shall I read to you?"

"Yes, do," said Rosa and Lucy, both at once.

"Well, I will, if Lucy will get my Natural History off my table."

Lucy jumped up in a moment, and ran for the book: the hall-lamp showed her the way until she got to the room door, and then, by the faint starlight, she easily found the volume. There were other books which Rosa would have preferred, and Harty was a very dull reader; but she listened patiently, and got quite interested at last in an account of an elephant that went mad in London, a favourite story with Harty.

Lucy was very sorry when bed-time arrived; but there was not a word to be said, for Mrs. Maxwell put the lamp in her hand, and bade her "Good night" most decidedly.

As Lucy entered her own pretty room, she thought of little Judy watching beside her dead mother in that poor cottage, and she wondered that it had never struck her before that God had surrounded her with so many blessings.

Judy's washing had not been very well done, and as Rosa thought best to send back the little frock as soon as possible, she was in haste to have it made clean.

After Lucy had gone to bed, she went to the kitchen with it in her hand. Old Betsy was sitting by the fire, looking very stupid and cross. Rosa was almost afraid to ask her to do what she had intended. She took courage, however, and said, "Betsy, I want you to wash this little frock for a poor boy who has no other to wear but the one he has on. I know you would be glad to do it, if you had seen the poor little fellow lying by his dead mother: he has nobody at home to wash his clothes now."

Betsy had looked very sour when Rosa commenced, but softened as she continued to speak, and when Rosa finished, she took the little frock in her hand, saying, "I suppose I shall ketch something, handling this thing, but I can't say no to you, for you are the image of your mother."

"Thank you, Betsy," said Rosa; "I hope I may be like my mother. You need not do the frock to-night; it will be time enough in the morning. The funeral is not till three o'clock to-morrow afternoon, and I can get Harty to take it down after school."

"I guess Master Harty will not be running for anybody," said Betsy to herself, as Rosa went up stairs; but she was wrong: Harty did go, and took with him, besides, a penny cake, that he had bought for Larry.

CHAPTER XII
THE VISITOR

Rapidly, happily, the weeks flew by at Dr. Vale's cottage: there seemed to be a new spirit at work there. Lucy no longer looked sad and drooping: there was always a bright face to welcome her return from school, and some one to listen to her account of the occurrences of the day. If her lessons were difficult, Rosa was always ready to explain them, and to encourage her to more persevering study. By degrees, Lucy was learning to share all her feelings with her sister. Sometimes Rosa found these confidences rather tiresome, but she never checked them, as she Was anxious that Lucy should speak to her without restraint, that they might be able to talk freely on the most important of subjects.

Many of Lucy's fears seemed to have passed away without effort as she became more cheerful; others she had been enabled to conquer by Rosa's kind advice; but the great secret of the new courage that she seemed acquiring, was found in the few words, "God is with me, God loves me," which were seldom far from Lucy's mind.

At first she could not help feeling that when she had done wrong, God had ceased to love her. Then Rosa would read to her passages from the Bible where the Saviour speaks of having come to save sinners, and would remind her, again and again, that she was God's own child.

"God made you, my dear Lucy," she would frequently say; "and He loves everything that He has made, and 'would not that any of His little ones should perish.' Christ has died that you may be forgiven; He has promised to receive all that truly come unto Him; His child you were made in Baptism, and His child you are glad to be; then why should you fear?"

"It seems so strange that God is willing to forgive me so often," Lucy would reply, "I can hardly believe it."

"It is, indeed, most wonderful; but for Christ's sake His poor erring followers are received, if they truly repent," would Rosa answer.

"I wish I could be perfect in a minute," said Lucy, one day; "I get tired of trying."

"When Christ has done so much for us that wo may share His happy home in heaven, we ought to be willing to stay here as long as He pleases, and strive to follow His example. If we prayed more earnestly for God to assist us, we should find it easier to do right; for God gives His Holy Spirit freely to them that ask Him. If you can constantly remember that God is with you, you will soon learn to turn to Him when you are tempted," answered Rosa.

Lucy thought that Rosa had no trouble to do right always; but it was a mistake. Many times hasty words came to Rosa's lips, and unkind thoughts were offered to her mind; but they wore followed so quickly by the effort to subdue them, and the prayer for aid, that they never were made known to those around her.

Cold winter weather had come: it seemed to make Harty only the more full of life and spirits. When he came in from the keen air, there was always a bustle in the circle round the fire. Sometimes he would lay his cold hands suddenly on Lucy's neck, and shout with laughter as she shivered and drew away; sometimes Rosa's cheeks got rubbed with a snow-ball until they were redder than usual; and almost always the noisy fellow was reproved by Mrs. Maxwell for bringing in so much snow or mud on his boots.

Yet Rosa was learning to love her rough brother very dearly, and she even fancied she could see some improvement in him. After a long talk with his sister, he would be more gentle and quiet for a few days; but soon some trifle would throw him into a passion, and all his goodness departed. He was so accustomed to speaking rudely to Lucy, that he never thought of it afterwards; yet he was mortified when in his fits of passion he had been unkind to Rosa.

She never seemed to retain any remembrance of his fault, but was ready to meet him pleasantly again as soon as his bad humour had passed away.

He could not help admiring her noble spirit; and every day he felt more and more sure that there was some strength in the principles that could keep a high-spirited girl like Rosa uniformly gentle.

By degrees Harty took less pleasure in teasing Lucy, and more happiness in her society. She had followed Rosa's hints, and tried not to be vexed and hurt by trifles, and really was becoming more interesting as she grew more cheerful and talkative.

Dr. Vale was still obliged to be very much away from home, but the time that he could spend with his family he greatly enjoyed; and he often rejoiced that Rosa had been brought home to throw around her such an atmosphere of sunshine.

Even Mrs. Maxwell had relaxed a little from her stiffness: she occasionally allowed Rosa to put Harty's room in order at first, and finally she gave up that charge entirely to her. This arrangement prevented much disturbance, for Rosa handled carefully the veriest trash, which she knew had value in Harty's eyes; and there were no more broken cobwebs to put him out of temper.

Often, when Mrs. Maxwell was weary, she found a comfortable chair placed for her by the fire; when her eyes were painful at night, unasked, Rosa would read the daily paper aloud. Such trifling attentions were very grateful to the faithful housekeeper, and it soon became a favourite joke with Harty to call Rosa "Mrs. Maxwell's pet."

As regularly as Saturday came, little Judy appeared, leading Larry by the hand, for he was now nearly two years old, and a fine healthy boy.

Lucy often wished that she could stay in the room with Rosa and Judy, but the latter could never attend to her sewing while her little brother was in her presence. She was constantly stopping to bid him say, "Thank ye" to the lady, or shame him for running about as if he were as much at home as the ladies.

Lucy found it very easy to amuse Larry, and before long she grew fond of him, and looked forward with pleasure to his Saturday visit.

With Harty's consent, and Mrs. Maxwell's valuable assistance, some of his old clothes were "cut down" for Larry, and he was warmly dressed in a good great-coat and cap, that delighted him exceedingly, though Judy could not help laughing when she first saw him in them.

Judy learned much more than the use of the needle from Rosa. As she sat sewing, Rosa taught her many sweet hymns and passages from Scripture, and led her to look to her kind Heavenly Father as a friend who would "never leave nor forsake her."

The short winter days and the long winter evenings soon passed away. One bright spring morning Lucy was looking at the hyacinths that were blooming beside the cottage wall, when she heard a footstep, and, turning round, she saw a stranger standing beside her. Once she would have started away like a frightened bird; but now she did not think of herself, but waited politely until the stranger should announce his errand.

"The flowers are peeping forth again; I see you love them," he said, cheerfully; "and what a place this is for birds; I never heard such a twittering. Are there any robins in the old nest at the bottom of the garden?"

"Oh yes, they have come," answered Lucy, wondering who could know so well about the robin's nest.

"We ought to be friends, Lucy," continued the stranger's pleasant voice, "for I could hush you when you were a baby, when nobody else could make you stop crying. You were a fat little thing then, and you are not so very much heavier now." And he jumped the little girl high in the air.

Lucy by this time had made up her mind, that whoever the stranger might be, she liked him.

"Can it be uncle Gillette?" she had once thought to herself; but she immediately decided that it was not he, as she had always imagined him very stern, with large black eyes, and the stranger's face was mild and cheerful, and his eyes were of a soft hazel.

"I have more little friends in the house," said the gentleman, and with Lucy's hand in his, he entered the door. Rosa was half-way down stairs; she caught one glimpse of the stranger, and then gave a flying leap, which nearly brought her to his side.

"Oh! uncle Gillette, I am so glad to see you," she said, as he bent to kiss her, apparently as delighted as herself.

Harty came out to see what was the cause of all this commotion, and was greeted with a cordial shake of the hand, and the address, "I hope Harty has not forgotten his old playfellow, uncle Gillette."

The children thought their father welcomed their uncle somewhat coldly; but they changed their minds when they found that he had been expecting him for several days, and had accompanied him from the station to the gate.

Lucy had supposed that she should be very much afraid of Mr. Gillette, as she knew that he was very learned and good; but she found him as mild and simple as a little child, and she was most happy to take the low stool he placed for her at his side, and look into his pleasant face, while she listened to his conversation.

She was heartily sorry when she heard him say that he was to leave on Monday morning, for as it was Saturday, they would have but a short visit from him.

There was no settled clergyman at Chatford at this time, the rector being absent for the benefit of his health. On this account a long time had passed since the children of the parish had been catechised in the church. There was therefore no small bustle among the little people when it was announced on the Sunday morning after Mr. Gillette's arrival, that the children would be called upon to recite the Catechism that afternoon, immediately after the service.

There was much buzzing and studying at noon; and many a boy was astonished that he had forgotten what was once so familiar to him, in the long interval which had passed since the last catechising.

Even Lucy was glad to study over what she called the "long answers," although she never failed to repeat them with her brother and sister every Sunday evening. She did not dare to lay her Prayer Book aside until Rosa had patiently heard her say the whole Catechism, and pronounced it perfectly learned.

Many young hearts that had palpitated with fear at the idea of reciting to a stranger, were reassured when the Rev. Mr. Gillette arose after the Evening Service, and said, "The children may now come up to the chancel."

Without a thought that any one was observing her, Lucy stepped out and joined the throng of boys and girls that were moving up the aisle. Julia Staples was tittering in the pew behind, and Judy M'Grath was walking at her side; but she did not see either of them; she felt that she was in God's holy temple, and about to perform a solemn duty, and she inwardly prayed that she might be able to understand and improve by Mr. Gillette's explanations.

The children were allowed to recite together, and their voices joined in a full chorus, as they answered correctly all the questions of the Catechism. Glances of triumph and congratulation passed from eye to eye as they finished, or not once had they faltered, even in the most difficult parts.

"What is the Catechism?" asked Mr. Gillette.

"It is a preparation for Confirmation," answered one of the boys.

"You have all recited the Catechism perfectly; are you then prepared to be confirmed?" said Mr. Gillette.

There was no answer for a moment, and all looked confused; at length there was a faint "No."

"I fear not," continued Mr. Gillette: "how, then, must you say this Catechism before you are ready to be confirmed?"

"We must speak it from the heart," said Judy M'Grath.

Some of the boys smiled at her Irish accent, but one glance from Mr. Gillette sobered them.

"Right! When do you take upon yourselves the promises made for you by your sponsors in Baptism?" he asked.

"At Confirmation," several replied.

"True," said Mr. Gillette, "at Confirmation you take these promises publicly upon yourselves. I see many before me," said he, looking tenderly about him, "who are too young for Confirmation, but hardly a child who is not old enough to make those solemn promises to God in private, and strive earnestly to keep them. Do not wait, my dear children, until you are old enough to be confirmed, before you promise to love and obey the Saviour who has redeemed you. Your sponsors laid you as infants on His bosom; turn not from Him with your first feeble footsteps. You were made members of Christ at Baptism; ask God this day to help you to live as the lambs of His flock. If you commence now to strive to keep your baptismal promises, Confirmation will indeed be, as it ought, a strengthening of you in all that is good, an assistance in leading that holy life which becomes the children of God, the members of Christ, and the inheritors of the kingdom of heaven.

"Let me ask you once more, Do you not believe that you are bound to believe and do as your sponsors promised for you? Let me hear that answer again, and may God give you strength to speak it from the heart."

"Yes, verily, and by God's help so I will; and I heartily thank our Heavenly Father that He has called me to this state of salvation, through Jesus Christ our Lord," was heard from the throng around the chancel.

Even those who stood nearest to Lucy could hardly hear her voice; no human friend saw her uplifted eye; but God, who seeth all hearts, accepted the vow she made in His holy temple, and she felt more fully than she had ever done before, that she was indeed the child of God.

Lucy was not the only child who had listened earnestly to Mr. Gillette. It was the last time that he ever addressed those children; but there will be those at the resurrection who will thank him for the words he spoke that day: good resolutions were then roused in young hearts, which strengthened until they became strong principles, which supported through life, sustained in death, and were perfected in heaven.

CHAPTER XIII
SICKNESS

All was changed at Dr. Vale's cottage on Monday noon: Mrs. Maxwell, Harty, and Lucy once more sat down to dinner by themselves. The doctor was with a distant patient, and Rosa had gone with Mr. Gillette, to pass a few days in the city.

Although Mr. Gillette had been with them so short a time, both Harty and Lucy were sorry to part with him; and they did not wonder at Rosa's strong attachment to their uncle.

Lucy felt very sad when it was first proposed that Rosa should leave home, although it was only for a few days; but she knew this was a selfish feeling, and struggled to overcome it. Early on Monday morning the packing of Rosa's trunk commenced. Lucy ran about to wait on her sister, and helped her in her preparations as cheerfully as if she herself were of the party; she even insisted upon lending her certain belts and ribbons which were the treasures of her wardrobe.

Harty was not up when the carriage came to the door; he had been called once, but had fallen asleep again. He thrust his tumbled head from the window, and bade his sister a hearty farewell as she drove from the door.

This little circumstance seemed to have put him in a bad humour for the day. He pushed away his plate at breakfast, declaring he would not eat a mouthful of such trash; although everything was very nice, and there were hot cakes, of which he was usually very fond. Notwithstanding Harty's ill-humours, he was a favourite with old Betsy, and she was always careful to send him up a good breakfast, even when he had been lazy.

At dinner, his temper did not seem to have improved. "How you do eat," he said to Lucy: "it takes away my appetite to see you stuff so. I will speak to father about it."

Poor Lucy looked up in surprise, for she was only quietly taking a moderate meal. Once she would have answered pettishly or begun to cry, but Rosa had taught her that a cheerful as well as a soft answer often turneth away wrath, and she smilingly replied, "Why, Harty, I shall not be a stout, rosy girl soon, unless I make good dinners. Do try some of this horse-radish, it will make you relish your dinner as well as I do."

"Pshaw!" exclaimed Harty, impatiently, "you need not try so hard to be like Rosa: you can never hit it; you are as unlike as an acorn to an apple."

Lucy blushed, and was glad that Mrs. Maxwell spoke to her just then, for she was hurt by her brother's rudeness, and tempted to make a hasty reply.

Mrs. Maxwell wanted a certain apron for a pattern, and Lucy ran for it as soon as dinner was over, little thinking that even Mrs. Maxwell had learned something from Rosa, and had spoken to her at that moment to change the conversation.

Lucy really felt sorry to see Harty come into the dining-room after tea, as if he intended to spend the evening there, for the frown was on his brow. She was about to ask him why he did not go to see John Staples, when she remembered that Rosa had said that John was a bad companion, and that sisters ought to do everything to make their home pleasant, even when their brothers were cross and disagreeable; for boys were often led into temptation when out of the house, from which they were safe when at home.

With these thoughts in her mind Lucy laid aside a mark which she was working for Rosa, and which she was anxious to finish before her return, and went for the chequer-board.

"Don't you want to beat me?" she asked gently of Harty.

"It is so easy to do that, I don't care for it," was his reply.

The little girl was not discouraged; she took out her scrap-book and pictures, and the bottle of gum-arabic, and placed them on the table. She knew Harty would be sure to take an interest in some new engravings which one of the school-girls had that day given her.

A spirited engraving of a wild horse caught his eye, and he soon was engaged in looking over the addition to the old stock, and in advising Lucy where to paste them. One of the engravings he claimed as his own. Lucy knew perfectly that he was mistaken, but she gave it to him without a word; and when he laughed at her awkward way of using the brush, she joined in the laugh, holding up her sticky fingers in a comical way.

Presently Harty put his head on the table, and fell fast asleep.

"Harty must be unwell," said Mrs. Maxwell, as she roused him from his heavy sleep, and told him he had better go up to bed.

Grumbling at being waked, he disappeared, without saying Good night to anybody.

Rosa's room looked lonely and deserted to Lucy as she passed it that night; and she wondered, as she put the lamp down on her own little table, where her sister was, and what she was doing.

That pretty room was a different place to Lucy from what it once was. She did not think of looking for robbers now; she had given that up long ago; and when she looked out of the pleasant window, the stars seemed like spirits, that told her of the power of the great God, who was her friend. She had ceased to hear mysterious noises in the orchard; the stillness of the night was only disturbed by the twittering of some restless bird, or the waving of the tender leaves in the soft wind; but Lucy felt no fear as she looked out upon the quiet scene. Once she had been afraid of ghosts, and often feared at night to see some white figure rise before her; but since she had learned to love the ever-present, invisible God, she felt safe from all harm, whether from spirits or evil men. Lucy liked to be alone now, that she might think about the gentle Saviour who was ever with her. To that Saviour she spoke in sincere prayer that night. Her brother was not forgotten: she prayed that God might watch over him and make him truly good, and as she did so there was not a harsh feeling in her heart towards him, notwithstanding his unkindness during the day.

In the middle of the night Lucy woke suddenly: she did not long doubt as to what had roused her, for the rain was falling in torrents, and soon there was a heavy clap of thunder, at almost the same moment that the room was lit by the glare of lightning. Lucy lay very still: she could not help feeling that there was some danger, but she was calm and peaceful. "The lightning is in God's hand, my Father's hand," she thought. "He will take care of me;" and she was soon almost asleep again. A loud groan made her start up in bed and listen. It was repeated, and seemed to come from Harty's room. Without a thought but of alarm for her brother, she slipped on her shoes, and throwing her little wrapper about her, she ran to him.

"What is the matter, Harty?" film asked, as she stood by his side.

"Go away! they'll not get me; I know where to hide," he muttered.

"Wake up, Harty," said Lucy, "there's nobody trying to catch you."

The lightning lit the room, and she saw that her brother's eyes were wide open, and that his cheeks were flushed. She took his hand; it was burning hot: he snatched it from her, saying, "Let me go, John, you don't play fair."

"Don't you know me, brother?" said Lucy, leaning over him.

"Oh yes, Thomas; tell Betsy to bake me some cakes," was his reply.

Poor Lucy! what should she do? She did not like to leave her brother to call Mrs. Maxwell; yet something, she knew, ought to be done for him immediately. At length she thought to knock on the wall, and wake Mrs. Maxwell, as her room was next to Harty's.

"What, afraid again?" said Mrs. Maxwell, as she saw Lucy standing by her brother's bed.

A groan from Harty, and a few muttered words, immediately drew her attention to him.

"I told you he was ill last night; why, how hot he is! Harty, what ails you?" said Mrs. Maxwell in a breath.

Harty could not tell what ailed him, for he was delirious with fever.

"What shall we do?" said Mrs. Maxwell, desperately: "your father won't be home till near morning, I know, and I am afraid to give any medicine, for he always scolds about my 'dosing the children.'"

"But Harty ought to have something done for him, I am sure," said Lucy.

"Well, we'll do what we can to put him in a perspiration," said Mrs. Maxwell. "I'll go to the kitchen and make him some hot drink, and get hot water for his feet, and may be that'll be the best thing till the doctor comes home." So saying, she disappeared with the light she had brought in her hand.

Lucy put on her brother's great coat, that lay on a chair; for the storm had cooled the air, and she was quite chilly. Thus equipped, she began to act the nurse as well as she could. Her first step was to light a lamp. Harty had a nice lucifer-box on his shelf: she felt carefully for it, and managed to find it without knocking down any of his treasures.

Not a thought of fear crossed her mind, although Mrs. Maxwell had gone to the kitchen in the basement, and there was no one near to aid her, if her brother should attempt in his delirium to injure her. Love to God made her trust in His protection; love to her brother made her forgetful of danger to herself while striving to be useful to him. She bathed his burning forehead, and moistened his parched lips, and often spoke to him tenderly, hoping he might answer her naturally. Sometimes, for a moment, she fancied he knew her, but as she bent to catch his words, some unmeaning sentence would convince her she was mistaken. How welcome was the sound of her father's footstep! Unconscious of any evil, Dr. Vale entered the house, and was hurried to Harty's bedside. Lucy watched his face as he felt her brother's pulse and noticed his other symptoms, and her heart grew sadder yet as she read his deep anxiety.

Mrs. Maxwell told him how fretful and indifferent to food Harty had appeared during the day, and of his unusual nap in the evening; and as she did so, Lucy felt grateful that she had borne pleasantly with her brother's ill-humour, which had, no doubt, been caused in part by disease. How painful her feelings would have been if she had treated him with unkindness, though with ever so great provocation! Children can never know how soon the illness or death of their friends may make them bitterly lament the slightest harshness towards them.

When Dr. Vale had given Harty such medicines as he thought most sure to give him relief, he for the first time noticed Lucy, who had kept by the bedside. Even in his sadness, he almost smiled at the funny little figure wrapped in the thick coat, with only the face visible, looking out from the nightcap.

"Go to bed, child; you can do no good here, and it will make you ill to lose your sleep," he said to her, gently.

"But, father," she pleaded, "I shall not sleep if I do go to bed; I can't bear to leave poor Harty."

"Mrs. Maxwell and I can do all that is needed for him to-night, my dear," said he, kissing her sorrowful face. "To-morrow we shall want you to run about and wait on us. Go, take some rest, like a good child, that you may be able to be useful in the morning."

With this motive to console her, Lucy went to her room. When there, all the fearful reality of Harty's illness came fully upon her. He might be taken from her, she thought, and at the very idea her tears flowed fast, and her heart throbbed with distress. Lucy did not long forget the heavenly Friend to whom she had learned to go in all her trials. Now she prayed earnestly to Him to spare her brother's life, or grant him his reason, that he might be able to realize his awful situation if he indeed must die. After this prayer she felt more composed, although very, very sad. At last she fell asleep, and did not wake until the sun was several hours high.

Her first thought in waking was of her brother. She stole gently to his door. Mrs. Maxwell was sitting beside him: she motioned to Lucy to go away, and made a sign that Harty was sleeping.

The sorrow and anxiety of that day would have been harder for Lucy to bear, if she had not been so busy. Mrs. Maxwell did not leave the sick-room, and Dr. Vale was there nearly all the time; but unwilling as he was to leave his son, he was obliged to visit other patients several times during the day.

Lucy was kept almost constantly in motion. She brought for Mrs. Maxwell what was needed from the surgery or the kitchen, and carried messages in all directions. She carefully placed a little chair by the door, and there she sat silently, to be ready whenever she might be wanted.

Lucy did not ask her father any questions, but she hoped from hour to hour to hear him say that her brother was better; but no such cheering words fell from his lips.

Towards evening he hastily wrote a letter, and said to Lucy, as he handed it to her to send to the post, "I have written to Rosa to come home immediately. Tell Patty to have a room ready for Mr. Gillette; he will return with her."

These words were full of dreadful meaning to Lucy. Harty must be very ill, she knew, or Rosa would not have been sent for. Throwing aside her usual quiet manner, she clasped her father round the neck and sobbed upon his bosom. "Dear, dear father," she whispered, "do you think Harty will die?"

"God may spare him," said Dr. Vale, his strong frame shaking with emotion, and the tears in his eyes.

Lucy had never seen her father so much moved before, and she felt sure that he had very little hope that her brother would be well again.

She ceased sobbing, and a strange calmness came over her. Every impatient or unkind word that she had ever spoken to Harty came back to her; and oh how solemnly she resolved, if he should recover, to be a better sister to him than she had ever been before! She tried to remember something that Harty had said which could make her feel sure that he would be happy in heaven, if he should die. She thought of the Sunday evening when he had bid her "Good night" so kindly, and joined in saying the Catechism; of the first Sunday that he had made a prayer on entering church; and of the many times that he had listened with interest while Rosa talked of the Saviour. But these recollections did not set her mind at rest. She knew that God had said, "My son, give me thine heart;" and she felt sadly sure that Harty had never, in sincerity, given his heart to God.

CHAPTER XIV
CONCLUSION

Rosa reached home on Wednesday morning. Her bright smile had vanished, and her sweet eyes looked sad and tearful; yet her step was firm and her manner calm. Lucy felt sure when she met her sister, that she had found support in this great trouble from that God who bids us "cast all our care on Him, for He careth for us."

When Rosa bent over Harty, and called him by name, he looked strangely at her, and, muttering, turned away. At first this was almost too much for her to bear; but by degrees she became accustomed to it, and commanded herself sufficiently to relieve Mrs. Maxwell from her post as nurse. Poor Mrs. Maxwell was quite worn out, and was very glad to take a little rest. Lucy had darkened her room, that she might sleep the better; and as soon as the tired woman had lain down, she stationed herself by the door to keep the hall as quiet as possible. Lucy found that she had been unjust to Mrs. Maxwell. She had always thought her a stern woman with a cold heart; but when she saw how tenderly she watched by Harty's bedside, she felt that she should always love her for it, and never call her cross again, when she found fault about trifles.

Mrs. Maxwell herself was surprised to find how deeply she had become attached to Dr. Vale's children. She had met with much misfortune and unkindness in the world; and when she came to live in Dr. Vale's family, she resolved to do her duty faithfully, and did not expect to love those around her or be loved by them. Although her severe manner had softened but little, by degrees she had become so fond of the children that she was only happy when doing something for them; and now her anxiety for poor sick Harty knew no bounds.

Several sad days of care and nursing passed by. Dr. Vale, Mrs. Maxwell, and Rosa, were with Harty by turns, day and night; and Lucy patiently waited on all until evening came, when she slept soundly from pure weariness.

Mr. Gillette was a comfort to all: he seemed truly a messenger from his Master in heaven, for there were ever sweet words of consolation on his lips.

He daily offered prayers in the room of the sick boy; and all who knelt with him rose up strengthened by trust in the God who "doeth all things well."

One day, when Harty had been ill a week, Rosa was sitting by him in silence, when, in a low, weak voice, he called her by name.

"My dear brother," she answered, very calmly, although she was much startled.

He took the hand she placed on his, and said, in a searching manner, "Am I very ill?"

"We hope you may get well, but you are in God's hands," was Rosa's reply.

To be in God's hands was not an idea of peace to poor Harty. He could not turn with loving trust in sickness to the God whom he had neglected in health. A pang darted through his heart, a pang of fear and remorse, more deep and painful than he had ever felt. He was to die with all the sins of his youth upon him! In his weak state this awful thought was too much for him, and his mind again wandered in delirium.

Rosa continued by his bedside in silent prayer. She did not again hear her name called, as she hoped, and she was forced to resign her place to Mrs. Maxwell, without having another sign of consciousness from her brother.

When it was again Rosa's turn to act as nurse, she found that there had been a decided change in Harty. He slept more calmly, and breathed more naturally. Dr. Vale came in when she had been sitting by the bed a few moments: a rapid examination served to show him that there was, indeed, cause for hope.

The joyful news spread through the household, and many thanksgivings went up to the God who dispenses sickness and health. Rejoiced as all were at the idea of seeing Harty once more in health, there was in every heart a deeper cause of gratitude: they might now hope that he would not be called to meet his Father in heaven while yet a disobedient, wandering child. Time might yet be given him to learn, to know, and love that Father, and walk in His holy ways.

When Harty was again conscious of what was going on around him, his father was with him. "Don't trouble yourself to think now, my dear boy," said Dr. Vale, soothingly. "I hope you will soon be much better; and I pray God that He will enable you to lead a new life. Lie still now, and you will soon fall asleep again, to wake much refreshed, I hope."

Harty's recovery was slow and tedious. He was very weak, and little inclined to talk. He seemed most contented when Rosa was singing to him some pretty hymn, and Lucy was sitting by him on the bed smoothing his hair, or fanning him gently.

His large eyes looked sunken and thoughtful, and his manner, once boisterous, was mild and gentle.

"Don't move for me again this morning, dear Lucy," he said one day; "your little feet must be very tired with running up and down stairs. When I get well I shall have to wait on you all the rest of my life to repay you for this kindness."

This was so unlike the old, exacting Harty, that it quite overcame little Lucy, and the tears were in her eyes as she answered, "I love to do anything for you, my dear brother. I want nothing from you but to get well as soon as you can, and look bright, and merry, and tease me as you used to do."

A sad smile crossed Harty's face, as he said, "I don't mean to do as I used to do in anything, Lucy. You will forget how unkind I was to you, won't you, pet? I don't think I shall be so any more."

Lucy's tears fell fast. Don't talk so, Harty," she said; "You were never unkind to me. I was a foolish little thing, and let everything worry me. Come, we won't talk any more; you look tired. Here is Rosa, she will sing, —

'Softly now the light of day,' —

while you take a nice little nap."

By degrees the colour came again to Harty's cheeks, and his limbs renewed their strength.

One calm Sunday evening, towards the end of June, he was sitting between his sisters, looking out at the evening sky.

"Let us have the Catechism once more," said Lucy; "it will seem like old times."

Rosa and Lucy began as usual together. Harty's voice was with them; and there was a deep solemnity in his manner as he pronounced the words, "Yes, verily, and by God's help so I will; and I heartily thank our Heavenly Father that He has called me to this state of salvation, through Jesus Christ our Lord; and I pray unto God to give me His grace that I may continue in the same unto my life's end."

His sisters felt that he spoke from his heart; and there was that joy in their hearts which the angels know over "one sinner that repenteth."

As the summer passed away, the cottage looked cheerful once more, as of old. The children again rambled in the woods or strolled in the orchard, and whenever their voices were heard the tones were pleasant and kindly.

True, they all had faults of character still to overcome, and were sometimes tempted to go astray; but there was in each heart an earnest wish to do right, and a spirit of love and forgiveness that kept them from all variance.

Mrs. Maxwell was still formal and particular; but she now had little cause for complaint, for Harty was so grateful for her watchful care during his illness, that he made many efforts to overcome his careless habits, and in a great measure succeeded.

"The dear boy forgot for once," she would sometimes say, as she hung his cap on the accustomed peg, or overlooked some act of heedlessness; for she felt that he was trying to please her, and she was the more ready to forgive him.

In the trying scenes by Harty's bedside Dr. Vale had been brought near in heart to his children. Now there was no subject on which he could not talk freely to them. He spoke to them of their mother, and told them anecdotes of her blameless life that were treasured up in their young hearts for loving imitation.

The blessed Saviour and the heaven He purchased for His faithful ones were often subjects for conversation in that happy family circle, and the doctor felt, as he looked into the faces of his children, that God had blessed their mother's prayers.

Uncle Gillette's letters were always welcomed with joy, and never read without cheering the young Christians in the path of duty.

Lucy had now nothing to fear: the sorrows of her timid childhood were over. Loving and cheerful, she made all happy around her. She had found a comfort for all sorrow, a Friend ever-present, a support for life and death, in Him who saith to the children of His love, "Fear not, little flock; for it is your Father's good pleasure to give you the kingdom."

www.ingramcontent.com/pod-product-compliance
Lightning Source LLC
LaVergne TN
LVHW041746190726
843493LV00008B/2476